*Love's Enduring
Promise*

Books by Janette Oke

www.janetteoke.com

Another Homecoming★
Tomorrow's Dream★

CANADIAN WEST

When Calls the Heart	*When Breaks the Dawn*
When Comes the Spring	*When Hope Springs New*

Beyond the Gathering Storm
When Tomorrow Comes

LOVE COMES SOFTLY

Love Comes Softly	*Love's Unending Legacy*
Love's Enduring Promise	*Love's Unfolding Dream*
Love's Long Journey	*Love Takes Wing*
Love's Abiding Joy	*Love Finds a Home*

A PRAIRIE LEGACY

The Tender Years	*A Quiet Strength*
A Searching Heart	*Like Gold Refined*

SEASONS OF THE HEART

Once Upon a Summer	*Winter Is Not Forever*
The Winds of Autumn	*Spring's Gentle Promise*

SONG OF ACADIA★

The Meeting Place	*The Birthright*
The Sacred Shore	*The Distant Beacon*

The Beloved Land

WOMEN OF THE WEST

The Calling of Emily Evans	*A Bride for Donnigan*
Julia's Last Hope	*Heart of the Wilderness*
Roses for Mama	*Too Long a Stranger*
A Woman Named Damaris	*The Bluebird and the Sparrow*
They Called Her Mrs. Doc	*A Gown of Spanish Lace*
The Measure of a Heart	*Drums of Change*

Janette Oke: A Heart for the Prairie
Biography of Janette Oke by Laurel Oke Logan

★with T. Davis Bunn

JANETTE OKE

Love's Enduring Promise

BETHANYHOUSE
MINNEAPOLIS, MINNESOTA

Published by Bethany House Publishers
11400 Hampshire Avenue South
Bloomington, Minnesota 55438

Bethany House Publishers is a division of
Baker Publishing Group, Grand Rapids, Michigan.

Printed in the United States of America

Library of Congress Cataloging-in-Publication Data

Oke, Janette, 1935-
    Love's enduring promise / by Janette Oke.
        p.   cm. — (Love comes softly ; bk. 2)
    ISBN 0-7642-2849-8 (pbk.)
    1. Davis family (Fictitious characters ; Oke)—Fiction. 2. Married people—Fiction.
3. Women pioneers—Fiction. I. Title. II. Series: Oke, Janette, 1935-   . Love comes softly series ; bk. 2.

    PR9199.3.O38L58   2003
    813'.54—dc22   2003014255

Dedicated with love to

Edward

Terry, Lavon, Lorne, and Laurel

—my wonderful family

JANETTE OKE was born in Champion, Alberta, to a Canadian prairie farmer and his wife, and she grew up in a large family full of laughter and love. She is a graduate of Mountain View Bible College in Alberta, where she met her husband, Edward, and they were married in May of 1957. After pastoring churches in Indiana and Canada, the Okes spent some years in Calgary, where Edward served in several positions on college faculties while Janette continued her writing. She has written over five dozen novels for adults and children, and her book sales total over twenty-two million copies.

The Okes have three sons and one daughter, all married, and are enjoying their dozen grandchildren. Edward and Janette are active in their local church and make their home near Didsbury, Alberta.

Visit Janette Oke's Web site at: *www.janetteoke.com.*

Contents

ONE

New Beginnings

Marty stirred restlessly. The dream had possessed her, and now she felt an uncontrollable shiver run through her body.

With her gradual wakefulness came an intense relief. She was here, safe and belonging, in her own bed.

Still, an uneasiness clung to her. It had been a horrible dream, so real and frightening. Why, she asked herself, did she even have this dream after all this time? And it had been so real—so very real.

She could feel the dream's frightening details close in about her again as she thought about it. The broken wagon, a howling blizzard pulling and tearing at the flapping canvas, and she, Marty, huddled alone in a corner, vainly clasping a thin, torn blanket about her shivering body in an effort to keep warm. Her despair at being alone was more painful than the cold that sought to claim her.

I'm gonna die, she had thought during the dream, *all alone. I'm gonna die*—and then, thankfully, she had awakened and had felt the warmth of her familiar four-poster and looked through the cabin window at a sky blessed with twinkling stars.

But she could not suppress another shiver, and as it passed through her body, a strong arm went about her, drawing her close.

She hadn't meant to waken Clark. His days were such busy

ones, full of farming and care of the animals, and she knew he needed his sleep. As she studied his face in the pale light from the window, she realized he wasn't really awake—not yet.

A flood of love washed over her. Whenever she needed assurance of his love, it was readily given to her, even from the subconscious world of sleep. This was not the first time that, even before he awakened, he had sensed her need and held her in his arms.

But wakefulness was coming to him now. He brushed a kiss against her loose hair and whispered, "Somethin' wrong?"

"No, I'm fine," she murmured. "I jest had me a frightenin' dream, thet's all. I was all alone an'—"

His arm tightened. "But yer not alone."

"No, an', Clark, I'm so glad—so glad."

As he held her close, she knew her shivering had ceased and the reality of the dream was gone.

She reached a hand to his cheek. "I'm fine now—really. Go back to sleep."

His fingers smoothed her hair, then gently rested on her shoulder. Marty lay quietly, and in a few moments Clark's breathing assured her that he was asleep again.

Marty had control of her thoughts now. With the terror of the dream pushed aside, now she used the quiet moments before the dawn to think through and plan for the activities of the day.

Over the winter months, every moment the community menfolk could spare from their own work had been given to felling and skidding logs. The families in the area felt strongly the need for a school for the educating of their children, and they knew the only way they would get one would be to build the structure themselves and find a teacher to go with it.

It would be a simple one-room affair, built near the creek on a piece of property donated by Clark and Marty Davis.

Gradually the piles of logs had grown. The men had been anxious to bring in the required number in front of the spring thaw, and then before the land would be beckoning to their plows, there would be time for a work bee or two.

The log count had been taken—the requirement filled. Tomorrow was the day set aside for the "school raisin'." The men hoped to complete the walls and perhaps even add the rafters. The building would then be completed through the summer as time allowed. By fall the children would have a school of their own.

Marty's thinking jumped ahead to the teacher. They still needed to find a teacher, and they were so difficult to locate and interest in coming out to the frontier. Would they build their school only to discover that they were unable to obtain a qualified teacher? No, they must all pray—pray that the little group working on the search would be fruitful, that their efforts of building the school would not be in vain, that a suitable teacher would be found.

Little Missie would not attend the school for its first term. She would be five come November and probably too young to join the others starting in the new school. Marty felt torn—she wanted Missie at home with her for another year. Still, in all the excitement over the new school, it was hard to not be actually involved with a child in attendance. She reminded herself again that Clark and she had decided Missie should wait—a hard decision, for Missie talked about the new school constantly.

At first the school had seemed so far into the future, but now here they were on the threshold of its "birthin'." The thought of it stirred Marty, and she knew she would be unable to go back to sleep, even though she should. It was too early to begin the day's work. Her moving about might waken the other members of the family.

She lay quietly, sorting out in her mind what food she would prepare for the school work crew on the morrow and what would need to be done in preparation today. She mentally dressed each of her children and even mentally noted which of the neighbor women she might want to have a chat with when the work would allow it. The opportunity to gather together, even if it meant hard work and extra effort, was something Marty treasured, and she knew the others of their community shared her anticipation.

The minutes seemed to tick by slowly, and finally her restlessness drove her from under the covers. She lifted herself carefully and slowly, for the child she carried made most movements cumbersome.

Jest another month, she reminded herself, *an' we will see who this is.*

Missie was hoping for a baby sister, but little Clare didn't care. A baby was a baby to his small-boy way of thinking; besides, a baby stayed in the house, and he, at every opportunity, marched along with his pa, trying to match his steps with Clark's. So Clare couldn't see a baby adding much to his world.

Marty slipped into her house socks and wrapped a warm robe about her. The little house was cold in the morning.

She went first to look in on the sleeping Missie and Clare. It was still too dark to see well, but through the light from the window their outlines assured her that they were covered and comfortable as they slept.

Marty went on to the kitchen and as quietly as possible lit the fire in the reliable old kitchen stove. Marty felt a kinship with her stove—almost like a man with his team, she reckoned with a little smile. The stove and she worked together to bring warmth and sustenance to this home and family. Of all the things their home held, the stove, she felt, was really hers.

The fire was soon crackling, and Marty put the kettle on to

boil and then filled the coffeepot. It would be a while before the stove warmed the kitchen and the coffee began to boil, so Marty pulled her robe about her for warmth and lifted Clark's worn Bible from the shelf. She'd have time to read and pray before the family began to stir.

She felt especially close to God this morning. The dream had made her aware again of how much she had to be thankful for, and the anticipation of the new school added to her feelings of well-being. As close and cared for as she felt with Clark, only God truly understood her innermost self. She was glad for the opportunity to pour it all out to the One she had come to know only recently.

Marty sat slowly sipping the hot coffee, enjoying its warmth spreading through her whole being. She felt refreshed now, both physically and spiritually. Again her eyes sought out the passage on the pages open in her lap. The verse had seemed meant especially for her at this particular time. *Be strong and of a good courage; be not afraid, neither be thou dismayed: for the Lord thy God is with thee whithersoever thou goest.*

The words were rich in promise and a comfort to her, particularly after her troubled dream. *Alone.* The word was a haunting one. She was so thankful she was not alone. Once more in deep humbleness and gratitude she acknowledged the wisdom of her Father in bringing Clark so quickly to her after the tragic death of husband Clem. She realized now that as soon as she had inwardly healed sufficiently to be able to reach out to another, Clark was already there, eager to welcome her. Why had she fought God's provision for her for so long—with every fiber of her being? Ma Graham had said it took time for the heart and the emotions to be restored, and Marty was sure that was the reason. Given that time—and Clark's gentle patience—she had been able to love again.

To love and be loved, to belong, to be a part of another's

life—what a precious part of God's plan for his creation, she thought as she poured herself another cup of coffee.

Had she ever been able to really tell Clark all she felt? Somehow to attempt putting it into words seemed never to do her true feelings the proper justice. Oh, she had tried to express it verbally, but words were so inadequate. Instead she sought to say it with her eyes, her actions. Indeed, her very being responded to him daily in a hundred ways.

The little life within her gave a sudden kick.

"An' you," Marty whispered, "you are one more expression of our love. Not jest the creatin' of ya, but the birthin' an' the raisin'. Thet's love, too. Yer special, ya know. Special 'fore we even know who ya are. Special because yer ours—God-given. God bless ya, little'un, an' make ya strong of body, mind, an' spirit. Might ya grow tall an' straight in every way. Make yer pa proud—an' he will be proud. Long as yer beautiful an' strong of soul—even if yer body should be weak or yer mind crippled—jest be upright of spirit. I know yer pa. Thet's what's most important to 'im. An' to yer ma, too."

A stirring from the bedroom interrupted Marty's inner conversation with her unborn child, and a moment later Clark appeared.

"Yer up early," Marty said, welcoming him with a smile. "Couldn't ya sleep, either?"

"Now, who could lay abed with the smell of thet coffee floatin' in the air? I declare, iffen those ladies anxious to catch themselves a man would wear the aroma of fresh-perked coffee 'stead of some Paris perfume, they jest might git somewhere."

They chuckled together, and Marty made to rise from her chair.

"Jest stay sittin'." Clark laid his hand on her shoulder. "I know where the cups are. Don't usually have the pleasure of a cup of coffee afore chorin'. Maybe ya could make this a habit."

He grinned companionably and reached for a mug. She knew he didn't really want her getting up any earlier, considering her busy days keeping up with two lively young'uns and another on the way.

Clark poured his coffee and came to the table where he sat across from her. He seemed to study her carefully, and Marty read love and concern in the look.

"Ya be all right?"

"Fine."

"Junior behavin'?"

Marty grinned. "When ya got up and came out here, I was jest sittin' here havin' a chat with her."

"*Her,* is it?"

"Accordin' to Missie, it daren't be anythin' else."

"Had me a bit worried there in the night."

"Thet weren't nothin' but a silly dream."

"Wanna talk 'bout it?"

"Not much to be sayin', I guess. It was the awful feelin' of bein' alone thet frightened me so. Don't rightly know how to be sayin' it, but, Clark, I'm so glad thet I never had to really be alone—even after I lost Clem. There was you an' Missie right away to fill my life. Oh, I know I shut ya out fer a time, but ya were there. An' Missie gave me someone to think about, a purpose, right away. I'm so glad, Clark. So thankful to God thet He didn't even give me a choice but jest stepped in an' took over, even when I wasn't thinkin' of Him."

Clark leaned across the table and touched her cheek. "I'm glad, too, Mrs. Davis." There was teasing in his eyes, but there was love there, too. "Never met 'nother woman thet could make better coffee."

Marty playfully brushed his hand aside. "Coffee—pawsh."

Clark's expression grew more serious. "Guess I was kinda hooked even 'fore I smelled the first potful. Never will fergit how little an' alone ya looked headin' fer thet broken-down wagon, tryin' so hard to hold yer head up when I knew thet inside ya jest wanted to die. The inside of me jest cried right along with ya. Don't s'pose there was another person there who understood yer feelin' better than I did. I ached to somehow be able to ease it fer ya."

Marty blinked away a tear. "Ya never told me thet afore. I thought thet ya were jest desperate fer someone to be carin' fer yer young Missie."

"True, I was, an' true, thet was what ya were s'pose to think. I tried hard fer the first couple of months to convince myself of it, too. Then I finally had to admit thet there was more to it than thet."

Marty reached out and squeezed his hand. "I got me a rascal," she teased.

"An' then ya up an' put me through the most miserable months of my life—wonderin' iffen ya'd ever feel the same 'bout me or iffen ya'd jest pack yer bags an' leave. Guess I learned more 'bout prayin' in those days than I ever had afore. Learned more 'bout waitin', too."

"Oh, Clark, I didn't even know," Marty whispered, choking up a little. She lifted his hand and placed a kiss on his fingers. "Guess all I can do is try to make it up to ya now."

He rose from his chair and bent over her, planting a kiss on her forehead. "Ya know—I jest might hold ya to thet. Fer starters, how 'bout my favorite stew fer supper—thick an' chunky?"

Marty wrinkled her nose. "A man," she said, "thinks the only way to prove yer love is to pleasure his stomach."

Clark rumpled her loose hair.

"I best be gittin' to those chores or the cows will think I've fergotten 'em."

He kissed her on the nose and was gone.

Ponderin's

The sun stretched and rose from its bed the following day, scattering pink and gold upon the remaining winter snow and the white-and-green fir trees. It promised to be a good day for the school raising. Marty breathed a prayer of thanks as she moved from her bedroom. She had been concerned that they might have another early spring storm, but here was a day just like she had hoped and prayed for. She apologized to the Lord for doubting His goodness, whether it rained or shone, and went quickly to the kitchen.

Clark had beat her to it this morning and had already left the house to do the chores. The fire he had built for her spread its warmth through the farm home. Marty hurried to get the breakfast on the table before the children appeared.

As she worked at the stove, stirring the porridge and making toast, a sleepy-eyed Clare walked into the room. His shirt was untucked and the suspenders of his overalls were twisted and fastened incorrectly. One shoe was on but still untied, and he carried the other under an arm.

"Where's Pa?" he questioned immediately.

Marty smiled as she looked at the tousle-haired boy.

"He's chorin'," she answered. "Fact is, he should be most done. Yer gonna have to hurry to git in on it this mornin'. Here, let me help."

She tucked in the shirt, fastened the suspenders correctly, and placed him on a chair to do up his shoes.

"This the day?" he wondered.

"Yep—this is the day. By nightfall we'll have us a school."

Clare thought about that for a while. He had already told Marty he wasn't sure he'd like school, but everyone else seemed excited about it. He smiled good-naturedly.

"Well, I better hurry," he said as he slid off the chair. "It's a good thing me not goin' ta school—Pa needs me."

Marty smiled. *Sure he does,* she thought. *Pa needs ya—needs ya to git in his way when he's feedin', needs ya to insist on draggin' along a pail thet's too big fer ya. He needs ya to slow his steps when he takes the cows back to pasture, needs ya to chatter at him all the time he's workin'.* She shook her head but the smile remained. *Yeah, he needs ya—needs yer love an' yer hero worship.* She bent to give the little boy a hug, then helped Clare into a warm coat, put his hands into his mittens and his cap on his head, and opened the door for him. He set out briskly to find his pa, Ole Bob prancing around him with delighted barks.

Marty returned to her breakfast preparations, glancing occasionally at the children's bedroom doorway. She'd have to call for Missie. She was a late sleeper and didn't bounce out of bed like Clare did each morning. Missie, too, liked adventure and discovery of what the day might hold, but she was willing to wait for it until a little later. Already she was a good little helper and was especially looking forward to assisting Marty with the new "little sister" on the way. For Missie's sake, Marty hoped the new baby would be a girl. She couldn't have loved Missie any more if she had been born of her own flesh and blood.

Marty set the table for their breakfast, wondering how many of the neighbor women were doing the same with similar excitement coursing through them at the thought of the new school. Their young'uns would not have to grow up ignorant just because their folks had dared to travel west to open up the frontier for farming and ranching. The children could grow up educated and able to take their place in the community—or other communities, if they would so choose.

Marty's thoughts turned to the two Larson girls, daughters of her friend Tina. Husband Jedd hadn't felt that the new school was all that necessary, calling it "plain foolishness—girls don't need edjecatin' anyway." But Tina Larson's eyes had silently pleaded that her girls be given a fair chance, too. They were getting older, thirteen and eleven now, and they needed the schooling before it got too late for them.

As she moved about her kitchen, Marty prayed that Jedd might have a change of heart.

In the midst of her praying, she glanced out the kitchen window and saw her *men* coming from the barn. Clark's normally long strides were restrained to accommodate the short, quick steps of little Clare. Clare hung on to the handle of the milk pail, sure that he was helping to carry the load, and chattered at Clark as he walked. Ole Bob bounded back and forth in front of them, assuming that he was leading the way and that without him the two would never reach their destination.

Marty swallowed a lump in her throat. Sometimes love hurt a little bit—but oh, such a precious hurt.

The Davis family was the first to arrive down by the creek, but then, they didn't have far to go, the land for the school having been set aside by Clark from his own homestead. Clark unhitched the team and began to pace out the ground, pounding in stakes as he went to mark the area for the school building.

Clare scampered around after him, grabbing up the

hammer as soon as it was laid down, handing out stakes, and being a general help and beloved nuisance.

An old stove had been placed in their farm wagon, and Marty busied herself preparing a fire and putting water on to heat. This stove didn't work nearly as well as the one in her kitchen, but it would be better than a campfire and would assist the ladies greatly in preparing a hot meal.

Missie pushed back her bonnet and let her light brown curls blow free. She enjoyed the feeling of the warmth of the sun on her head as she moved the team to a nearby clump of trees, where she tied them and spread hay for their breakfast.

Soon other wagons and sleighs began to arrive, and the whole scene took on a lively, excited atmosphere. Children ran and squealed and chased. Even Clare was tempted away from dogging his father's activities.

The women chattered and called and laughed as they greeted one another and fell in with the meal preparations.

Businesslike, the men began eyeing logs, organizing and choosing those best suited for footings, and mentally sorting the order in which the logs should be used. Then the axes went to work. Muscled arms placed sure blows as chips flew, and strong backs bent and heaved in unison as heavy logs were raised and placed. Marty noted with some pride Clark's acknowledged leadership among the men and their respect for him.

It was hard work, made lighter only by the number who shared it and the satisfaction that it would bring. An occasional hearty laugh or shared chuckle broke through the sounds of the work itself. And soon the shape of their schoolhouse was clearly seen as the walls gradually grew with each log set in place.

The early spring sun seemed almost hot, and the workers discarded jackets as their bodies grew warm from effort.

The old stove cheerily did its duty—coffee boiled and large kettles of stew and pork and beans began to bubble, spreading their welcome aroma throughout the one-day camp.

A child running by stopped in midstep to sniff hungrily and ask if dinner was ready yet, and a man, heaving a giant log, called over his shoulder to find out how soon the meal would be set out. At the stove, the woman who stirred the pot called that he should hold his horses, and she gave the little boy a smile and pat and admonished him to run along, no doubt imagining her child doing sums at a yet unseen blackboard.

The sun, the logs, the laughter—but most of all, the promise—made the day a good one. They all would go home weary yet refreshed—bodies aching but spirits uplifted. Together they would accomplish great things, not just for themselves, but for future generations. They had given of themselves, and many would reap the benefits.

Marty and Clark thought Ben Graham said it best as the group stood gazing at the new structure before turning teams toward home.

"Kinda makes ya feel tall like."

THREE

Little Arnie

Marty forced herself to set about getting supper. Clark would soon be in from the field and, thankfully, chores would not take him long.

In the sitting room Missie was busy bossing little brother Clare.

"Not thet way—like this!" Marty heard her exclaim in disgust.

"I like it this way," Clare argued, and Marty felt sure he'd get his own way. The boy had a stubborn streak—like her, she admitted ruefully to herself.

She stirred the pot to be sure the carrots were not sticking to the bottom and crossed mechanically to the cupboard to slice some bread. She wasn't herself at all—and she knew the reason.

She glanced nervously at the clock and held her breath as another contraction took hold of her. She really must get off her feet. She hoped Clark would be back soon.

As the contraction eased, Marty moved on again, placing the bread on the table and going for the butter.

She was relieved to hear the team arrive to Ole Bob's welcome and proceed on to the barn.

Clare must have heard the team, too, and ran through the kitchen, no doubt happy to be released from Missie's demanding play and return to a world where men worked together without interference from the womenfolk. Marty shook her head and chuckled in spite of herself as he grabbed his jacket from a hook and excitedly shoved an arm in the wrong sleeve. He would later discover his mistake and correct it as he ran, Marty knew.

Chores did not take long and Clark was soon in, bringing a foaming pail of milk that Clare assisted in carrying.

Marty dished up the food and placed it on the table as the "menfolk" washed in the outside basin. She sank with relief into her chair at the table and waited for the others to take their places.

Clark finished the prayer and began to dish food for himself and Clare. He glanced at Marty, then stopped suddenly and looked steadily into her face.

"What's troublin'?" he asked quietly.

She managed a weak smile. "I think it's time."

"Time!" he exclaimed, setting the potatoes on the table with a thump. "Why didn't ya say so? I'll get the doc." He was already on his feet.

"Sit ya down an' have yer supper first," Marty told him, but he was shaking his head before she could finish.

"Best ya git yerself to bed," he said, then turned to the children. "Missie, watch Clare." He looked into the little girl's face. "Missie, the time's close now fer the new baby. Mama needs to go to bed. Ya give Clare his supper an' then clear the table. I'm goin' fer the doc. I won't be long, but ya'll have to be a big girl and take care of things 'til I git back. If yer ma needs anything, ya get it for her, ya hear?"

Missie nodded solemnly.

"Now," Clark said, assisting Marty to her feet, "into bed with ya, and no arguin'."

Marty allowed herself to be led away. Bed was the thing that she wanted most—and second to that, she suddenly realized, was Ma Graham.

"Clark," she asked as he pulled back the quilt for her, "do we hafta get the doc?"

"'Course," he responded, stopping to look at her. "Thet's what he's here fer."

"But I'd really rather have Ma, Clark. She did fine with Clare, and she could—"

"The doc knows what to do iffen somethin' should go wrong. I know Ma has delivered lotsa babies, and most times everythin' goes well, but should somethin' be wrong, Doc has the necessary know-how and . . . and all."

A tear slid down Marty's cheek. She had nothing against the doc, but she wanted Ma.

Don't be silly, she told herself, but the thought remained, and as the next contraction seized her, the desire for Ma to be with her grew.

Clark handed her a nightie from the peg behind the door and helped her slip out of her dress and into the soft flannel gown.

He tucked her in and assured her with a kiss that he'd be right back. Marty noted his pale face and his quick, nervous movements. He left the room almost on the run, and a moment later Marty heard the galloping hoofbeats of the saddle horse leaving the yard.

From the kitchen came the voices of the children. Missie was still bossing Clare, telling him to hurry and clean his plate and to be very quiet 'cause Mama needed to rest so she could get the new baby sister.

Marty wished she could sleep, but of course none came as the contractions steadily increased in strength and frequency.

Missie rather noisily cleared the table, though Marty could tell she was trying to do it quietly. Then it sounded like she was busy putting Clare to bed. He protested that it was not bedtime yet, but Missie refused to listen and eventually won, to Marty's surprise and relief. Clare was bedded down for the night.

Missie poked her head into the bedroom to report on things, and fortunately it was between contractions, so Marty was able to converse normally with her. Marty hugged her with one arm, thanked her for her help, and directed the little girl to get herself into bed. Missie nodded solemnly, then obediently went along to do her mother's bidding.

The moments, then the hours, crawled by slowly. The contractions were awfully close together now and harder to bear without crying out.

Ole Bob barked and Marty, relieved, wondered at the doc getting there so quickly. But soon it was Ma who bent over her.

"Ya came," said Marty in disbelief and thankfulness. Tears immediately and unashamedly ran down her cheeks. "How did ya know?"

"Clark stopped by," Ma answered. "Said ya was needin' me."

"But I thought he was goin' fer the doc."

"He did. The doc will do the deliverin'. Clark said ya needed me jest fer the comfortin'." Ma smoothed back Marty's hair. "How ya doin'?"

Marty managed a wobbly smile. "Fine . . . now. I don't think it'll be as long this time as with Clare."

"Prob'ly not," Ma responded. She patted Marty's arm. "I'll check on the young'uns and get things ready fer the doc. Call iffen ya need me."

Marty nodded. "Thank ya," she said. "Thank ya fer comin'. I'll be fine . . . now."

Ma came and went, and then Marty was dimly aware of more voices joining Ma's in the kitchen. The words floated on the air toward her, and then Doc was beside the bed, talking to Ma in low tones, and Clark was bending over her, whispering words of assurance.

Marty was rather hazy about the rest of it until she heard the sharp cry of a newborn.

"She's here," Marty murmured quietly.

Doc's booming voice answered her.

"*He's* here. It's another fine son."

"Missie will be disappointed," Marty almost whispered, but Doc heard her.

"No one could be disappointed for very long over this boy. He's a dandy," and a few minutes later the new son was placed beside her. In the light of the lamp, Marty could see he was indeed "a dandy," and love for the new wee life beside her spread through her being like warm honey.

Then Clark came, beaming as he gazed at his new son and placing a kiss on Marty's hair.

"Another prizewinner, ain't he, now?" he said proudly. Marty nodded and smiled wearily.

Clark left, soon to return with a sleepy child in each arm. He bent down.

"Yer new brother," he whispered. "Look at 'im sleepin' there. Ain't he jest fine?"

Clare just stared big eyed.

"A boy?" Missie asked, sounding incredulous. "It was s'posed to be a girl. I prayed fer a girl."

"Sometimes," Clark began slowly, "sometimes God knows better than us what is best. He knows what we want might not be right fer us now, so sometimes, 'stead of givin' us what we asked Him fer, He sends instead what He knows is best fer us. Guess this baby boy must be someone special fer God to send him instead."

Missie listened carefully; then a smile spread over her face as the baby stretched and yawned in his sleep.

"He's awful cute, ain't he?" she whispered. "What we gonna call him, Pa?"

They named the baby Arnold Joseph and called him Little Arnie right from the first.

Clare seemed to find him a bit boring and complained that "Arnie don't *do* nothin'," though he would have defended him to the death. Missie fussed and mothered and wondered aloud why she'd ever felt a sister would've been any better.

Things settled down again to a comfortable routine. The crops and the gardens were planted. And Marty was going from early morning till late into the evening, for the new baby, along with the joy, also brought more work. Marty's days were full indeed—full, but overflowing with happiness and love.

FOUR

Visits

By fall of that year, Baby Arnie had grown steadily into a healthy and strong little boy. He had firmly established his rightful spot in the family, laughing and cooing his way into their hearts. He ignored Missie's instructions about the proper way to crawl and scooted around on his tummy.

When the crops were harvested, Clark declared the year's yield the best ever.

Marty somehow managed to keep up with the produce of her garden. Having Missie's helpful hands to entertain Arnie and keep an eye on Clare was greatly appreciated.

The only disappointment that fall was the new school. Over the busy summer months the men had found enough time to shingle the roof, install the windows, and put in the floor. A potbellied stove had been ordered and installed and simple desks had been built. The area farmers had each contributed to a pile of cordwood that stood neatly stacked in the yard. A crude shelter for the farm horses and the necessary outbuildings had been erected. Even the chalkboards were hung—but the school stood empty and silent. In spite of the diligent work done by the search committee, no teacher had been located.

Marty had lain awake restless and fretful more than one night because of it. It seemed so unfair that they would dream and work so hard to construct the fine little building only to have it stand vacant and the children left another year without formal education. Now the talk was of next year, but next year seemed an awful long time to wait. Especially for youngsters such as the Larson girls for whom opportunity for schooling was slipping away.

Marty was busy canning one morning when she heard the sound of an approaching team. With neighbors some distance away, visitors were all too few and very welcome. She wiped her hands on her apron and looked out the window to see Clark greeting Wanda Marshall and taking the team for her.

When Wanda headed for the house, Marty was immediately aware of her vegetable-spattered apron and her work-stained hands. She quickly threw the apron from her and drew a clean one from a drawer. Tying it about her as she went to the door, she could feel a smile already turning up the corners of her mouth.

She welcomed Wanda with a glad embrace, and both began to talk at once in their eagerness for a visit.

"I'm so glad thet ya came," Marty said. " 'Scuse my messy kitchen. Cannin', ya know."

"Don't ya mind," Wanda assured her. "I shouldn'ta come at such a busy time, but I just couldn't stay away. I just had to see you, Marty."

"Don't ya ever wait fer a time thet's not busy. My land, seems all the days are busy ones, an' I sure do need me a visit with a friend now an' then."

Marty supposed she should wait and let Wanda tell her news, but the glow on her face prompted Marty to question further. "But what's yer news? I can see yer fairly burstin'."

Wanda chuckled—almost a girlish giggle, Marty thought. She had never seen Wanda look so happy.

"Oh, Marty!" Wanda said. "That's right, I'm fairly bursting." Then she laughed, took a deep breath, and rushed on,

"I've just been to see Dr. Watkins. I'm going to have a *baby!*"

At Marty's exultant "Oh, Wanda!" she continued her report.

"Dr. Watkins says he sees no reason why I shouldn't be able to keep this one. No reason why it shouldn't live. Cam is so excited—says our son is going to be the handsomest, the strongest, the smartest boy in the whole West."

"Well, I'm guessin' Clark might have himself somethin' to say about thet," Marty laughed.

Wanda laughed, too. "When I asked him, 'What if it's a girl?' he said she would be the prettiest, the sweetest, and the daintiest girl in the whole West. Oh, Marty, I'm so happy I could just cry." And she did.

Marty went to put her arms around her, and they cried together, unashamed of the tears of joy that trickled down their cheeks.

"I'm jest so happy fer ya, Wanda," Marty finally was able to say. "An' with Doc here, everythin' will go all right, I'm jest sure. Ya'll finally have thet baby you've been wantin' so bad. When will it be?"

Wanda moaned, "Oh, it seems so far away yet. Not until next April."

"But the months will go quickly. They always do. An' ya can have the winter months to be preparin' fer 'im. Sewin' and quilting an' all. It'll make the winter sech a happy time. It'll go so fast ya'll find it hard to be doin' all ya want."

"I hope so. Marty, can you show me the pattern for that sweater Arnie was wearing last Sunday? I'd like to make one."

"Sure. Ya'll have no problem at all crochetin' thet."

Over coffee and sugar cookies, Marty and Wanda worked out the pattern—Wanda taking notes as Marty showed her the sweater and explained the crochet stitches.

The afternoon went quickly, and when Arnie and Clare

awoke from their naps, Wanda said she must be on her way.

Missie was sent to ask Clark if he would bring Wanda's team. He complied at once, and with another embrace and well wishes, Wanda was on her way home.

Marty walked back to the grain bin with Clark. "Wanda had the best news," she enthused. "She is finally gonna have thet baby she wants so badly. She's so excited. Oh, I pray thet everythin'll be okay this time."

Marty could tell Clark was pleased for Wanda. She went on, "An' Cam says iffen it's a boy, it'll be the smartest, handsomest, and best in the West, and iffen it's a girl, the prettiest. I told her you might give him some argument on that," and the two laughed together.

Then Clark's eyes became thoughtful.

"Ya prob'ly don't know Cameron Marshall too well yet, do ya?"

"I've hardly met the man—only seen 'im a few times at neighborhood meetin's. Why?"

Clark's expression became even more serious. He said, "He's a rather strange man." He paused a moment. "It's jest like Cam to feel thet his boy's gotta be the smartest, his girl the prettiest. Thet's like Cam." He waited a moment. "I think thet's the reason he married Wanda. He figured she was the prettiest girl he'd ever laid eyes on—so she jest had to be 'his.' The problem with Cameron Marshall is the importance he puts on 'mine's the best.' I 'member one time Cam saw a fine horse. He jest had to have it 'cause he figured it a little better'n any other horse in these parts. Sold all his seed grain to git thet horse. Set him back fer years, but he had him a better-lookin' horse than anybody 'round about. Guess he figured it was worth it.

"Ever notice his wagon? All painted up an' with extry metal trimmin's. Could have had a bigger place to live. Men of the neighborhood figured on being neighborly a few years back and helped him log so's he could build. 'Stead, he saw thet wagon, so he sold the logs an' bought it—an' he an' Wanda still live in thet one little room. The way Cam sees it, a house belongs to the woman, not the man. Often wished he'd take him a notion thet he had to have the best house, too—might find 'im a way to git one. Sure would be easier fer Wanda—an' now with a baby comin', they sure do need more room."

Clark was looking off at the distant hills as he finished. Marty had never known before what kind of a man Cameron Marshall was. She felt helpless and wished there was something she could do to help her friend.

Clark mused, "Often wondered what would make a man feel so unsure of himself like, thet he had to prove himself by gittin' *things*. Somethin' deep down must be troublin' Cam to have made 'im like he is."

Clark took a deep breath and seemed to bring himself back from a long way off. "Sure do hope thet the young'un be a dandy, or it's gonna be awful hard on his pa."

He turned to face Marty and smiled then. "Didn't mean to put a damper on yer good news. I'm sure Cam will have reason to be proud—an' Wanda—I'm real happy fer Wanda. It'll wake her life up to have a baby in it."

―――――――

The day held a chill with reminders that winter was around the corner. As Marty packed a box with bread, soup broth, vegetables, and molasses cookies, she was thankful no wind was blowing.

Word had come that morning that Mrs. Larson was ill. It sounded like something far more serious than a common cold or flu, and Marty felt she should go and see her neighbor, even though the cold wind was rather daunting.

Clark did not like to see her go alone, but with the fact that

Missie was far too young to be left in charge of Clare and Little Arnie, there was nothing for him to do but remain at home with the children.

Marty dressed as warmly as she could. Then, carrying her box with her, she went out to where Clark waited with the team.

"Don't let yerself to be kept over-late," he cautioned. "An' should it start to really blow, head home quick like."

Marty promised, tucked the blanket carefully around herself, and started off.

When the rather unkempt Larson homestead came into view, Marty noticed only a tiny wisp of smoke rising from the chimney of the cabin.

No one met her in the yard to assist her with the team, so she tethered Dan and Charlie to a nearby post and hurried, with her box, to the house.

There was a stirring at the window, and the tattered curtain fell back into place as she approached. Her knock was answered by the younger daughter, Clae, who quietly motioned her in.

Her sister, Nandry, was washing dirty dishes in a pan of equally dirty water. A stubby broom leaning against the table indicated to Marty that Clae had been making an effort to sweep the floor.

Well, at least they are trying, Marty thought with thankfulness. After greeting the girls, she turned to the almost-cold stove. The room was cold, too, and sent shivers through her, in spite of the fact she had not yet removed her coat.

She opened the lid of the stove to observe one lone piece of wood smoldering in the firebox.

"Where's yer wood?" she asked hopefully.

Clae answered, "Is none. Pa didn't get it cut, and we can't split it."

"Do ya have an axe?"

"Yeah . . . sort of."

Marty discovered what the "sort of" meant when she went out to the scattered heap that made up their meager winter supply. Never had she seen such a dull and chipped tool. With a great deal of effort she was able to chop enough wood to take the chill off the house.

After she had built up the fire and placed a kettle on to boil, she went in to see Mrs. Larson.

The woman lay huddled under some blankets on a narrow bed in the second room of the small cabin. Marty was relieved to see that at least clothing was not strewn all over the room. Then she realized with despair that probably everything they owned was on their backs, in an effort to keep out as much of the cold as possible. Mrs. Larson lay white and quiet beneath the scant covers.

Why didn't I think to bring a heavy quilt? Marty reprimanded herself, and even as the thought went through her mind, she saw the shiver that passed through Mrs. Larson. Marty stood close to the bed, reaching out to gently smooth the hair back from the thin white face.

"How are ya?" she whispered.

Mrs. Larson attempted an answer, but it was muted and low.

"I'll git ya some warm broth right away," Marty said and hurried back to the kitchen. She put the broth on to heat, then went out to the sleigh and returned with the blanket she had tucked around herself for the drive over. She warmed the blanket at the stove before she took it in to Mrs. Larson and wrapped it close about the shivering body.

The broth was soon warm, and Marty asked Clae for a dish and a spoon. She took the bread from the box and handed it to the girl.

"Why don't you an' Nandry have ya some broth while it's hot, an' some bread to go with it?" she said.

The hungry looks in the girls' eyes told her they would do so eagerly.

Marty carried the hot broth to Mrs. Larson. She realized the woman was already too weak to feed herself and hoped she would not object to being spoon-fed. There was no need to worry. Mrs. Larson accepted the food with thankfulness showing in her eyes.

"The girls . . ." she whispered.

"They're eatin'," Marty assured her quickly, and Mrs. Larson looked relieved.

Marty chatted quietly as she spooned. "I'm so sorry thet yer down. I didn't hear of it 'til today. Jedd should have let us know, an' we could've been over to help sooner.

"Nice thet ya got those two fine girls to be helpin'. When I came, Nandry was washing up the dishes an' Clae sweepin' the floor. Must be a great comfort to ya—them girls."

Mrs. Larson's eyes took on a bit more life, and she nodded slightly. Marty knew how she loved her girls.

"Must be a real tryin' time fer ya. A woman jest hates to git down—hates to not be carin' fer her family. Makes one feel awful useless like, but God, He knows all 'bout how ya feel— why yer sick. There's always a reason fer His 'llowin', though we can't always see it right off like. I'm sure there's a good reason fer this, too. Someday, maybe we'll know why."

The broth was almost gone, but Mrs. Larson feebly waved the remainder aside. Marty didn't know if she was full or just tired. Then Mrs. Larson spoke. Slowly at first, but gradually her words poured one over the other, tumbling out in quick succession in a need to be said. She breathed heavily, and the effort of speaking cost her dearly, but she seemed determined to get it out.

"My girls," she said, "my girls never had nothin', nothin'— thet's not what I want fer my girls. Their pa, he's a good man, but he don't understand 'bout girls. I been prayin'—prayin' thet somehow God would give 'em a chance. Jest a chance, thet's all I ask fer. Me—I don't matter now. I lived my life. Yet I ain't sayin' I'm wantin' to die—I'm scared to die. I ain't been a good woman, Marty. I got no business askin' God fer nothin', but I ain't askin' it fer me—only my girls. Do ya think God hears my prayers, Marty? I wouldn't 'ave even dared to pray, but my girls, they need—" She finally broke off with a sob.

Marty caressed the thin hand grasping the blanket.

" 'Course He hears," she said with deep conviction.

Mrs. Larson looked as though a great weight was being lifted from her.

"Could He show love to young'uns of a sinful woman?" Her eyes pleaded that the answer be reassuring.

"Yes," Marty said slowly. "He loves the girls, an' He will help 'em. I'm sure He will. But, Mrs. Larson, He loves you, too, an' He wants to help you. He loves ya, He truly does. I know thet yer a sinner, but we all are no different. The Book says thet we all be sinnin' an' hangin' on to our sin like it's somethin' worthwhile keepin', but it's not. We gotta let go of it, and God will take it from us an' put it there in thet big pile of sin thet Jesus took on himself the day He died. It isn't our goodness thet makes us fittin' to share heaven with Him. It's our faith in Jesus. We jest—well, we jest say 'thank ya, Lord, fer dyin', an' clean me up on the inside so's I'll be fittin' fer yer heaven'—an' He will. He takes this earth-soiled soul of ours an' He cleans and polishes it fer heaven. Thet's what He does, an' all—jest in answer to our prayer of askin'." Marty smoothed the tangled hair back from the feverish brow. "Do ya want to pray, Mrs. Larson?"

The woman looked surprised. "I've never prayed. Not fer myself—jest fer my girls. I wouldn't know what to say to Him."

"Ya said it to me," Marty reminded her gently. "Jest tell

Him thet yer done hangin' on to yer sins—thet ya don't want to carry 'em anymore, an' would He please git rid of 'em fer ya. Then thank Him, too—fer His love an' His cleanin'.'"

Mrs. Larson looked hesitant but then began her short prayer. The faltering words gradually gathered strength and assurance. When Marty opened her tear-dimmed eyes, she was met by a weak yet confident smile and equally teary eyes.

"He did!" Mrs. Larson exclaimed in a hoarse whisper. "He did!"

Marty squeezed Mrs. Larson's hand and wiped the tears from her own cheeks.

" 'Course He did," she affirmed. "An' He'll answer yer other prayer, too. I don't know how He'll manage it, but I'm sure thet He will."

She stood up. The sun was quickly moving to the west, and she knew she must be on her way home. "Mrs. Larson, I gotta go soon. I promised Clark I'd not be late, but there's somethin' I want ya to know. Iffen anythin' happens to ya—an' I'm hopin' ya'll soon be on yer feet again—but iffen anythin' does happen, I'll do my best to see thet yer girls git thet chance."

Mrs. Larson was silent. She seemed to be holding her breath, and then Marty realized she was too deeply moved to speak—save to her newly found God.

Again the woman's eyes filled with tears. "Thank ya, oh, thank ya!" she finally managed to say, over and over.

Marty touched her hand lightly and turned to go. She had to hurry home so there would be enough time for Clark to get back to the Larson homestead with a load of firewood and warm quilts.

F I V E

Exciting News

Marty finished patching a pair of Clare's overalls and laid them aside. It was too early to begin supper. She picked up another item of mending and let her mind slide over some of the events of the past few months.

She had gone several times to visit Mrs. Larson. Ma Graham and other neighbor women helped out often, as well, nursing the woman and caring for the needs of the family. Though Mrs. Larson rested contentedly in her newfound inner peace, she continued to weaken, and though none of them expressed it in words, Marty knew they were fighting a losing battle. The doc had been called, too, and he silently shook his head and encouraged them to keep her as comfortable as possible.

The children's laughter about something or other as they played near the warm stove pulled Marty's thoughts away from Mrs. Larson's illness to more cheerful things.

Spring would soon be upon them, and with its coming two new babies would be welcomed to their neighborhood—in April. Marty was very happy for the new mothers-to-be and prayed that all would go well.

The first to arrive would be Wanda's. She, who had already lost three children and wanted a child so badly, deserved to have this happiness. Now with a doctor available, Wanda had been given the confidence to hope this time would go well.

"Please, God, let it be all right for Wanda," Marty prayed many times a day.

The second baby was Sally Anne's. This first grandchild for Ben and Ma would be very special. Sally Anne, too, had hoped to be a mother earlier but had not carried her first baby to full term. Now the days of her delivery were very near at hand and things seemed to be going well this time. Marty knew that Sally Anne wasn't the only one counting the days.

As Marty mulled over the promise of new young lives that the month ahead would bring, her eyes turned to her own small ones as they played contentedly near by.

Missie was dressing a kitten in doll clothes. After much arguing and persuading on Missie's part, Marty had finally agreed to allow one small barn cat in the house. It was named Miss Puss by Missie and treated like a baby. Never had a kitten had more love and fondling than Miss Puss. Marty wondered if Miss Puss might have welcomed a few moments of peace.

Clare was piling blocks in an effort to construct a barn. The blocks would periodically fall on the unfortunate pieces of broom straw that were his farm animals, and then he would need to start over again.

Arnie, who could now sit alone, watched Clare intently, looking particularly fascinated by the noise created when the blocks came tumbling down. This would bring gurgles of delight, and his round little body would rock back and forth with excitement.

Clare dutifully explained to young Arnie which straws were the horses, which the cows, the calves, and the hogs. Arnie listened wide-eyed and squealed in response.

At the sound of Ole Bob, the room came alive. Clark had returned from town. Marty hadn't expected him for another hour. She got up quickly and checked the clock to see if she had misread the time. No, it was indeed early.

Clare jumped up from his spot on the rug. "Pa's home!" he shouted, letting his building blocks fall where they may, unmindful of the damage done to the straw horses and cows.

Marty started to call him back to pick up the toys, then changed her mind. He could pick them up when he came in for supper. It was important to him—and to Clark—that he now greet his pa.

Missie, too, holding carefully the blanketed kitten, headed for the door.

"Boy, I'll bet Arnie's sad!" Clare yelled as he ran through the kitchen.

"Whatcha meanin'?" Marty had to call after him to be heard.

"He can't run," the fleeing boy flung back over his shoulder and was gone, the door slamming behind him.

Marty smiled and went for Arnie, now deserted on the rug.

"Are ya sad?" she asked the baby as she lifted him up.

Arnie didn't look sad—maybe a bit puzzled at all the sudden bustling about, but otherwise content. A happy smile spread over his face. Marty kissed his cheek and walked to the kitchen window.

She had expected to see Clare and Missie hitching a ride with Clark to the barn, so she was surprised when all three were coming up the path to the house together. The youngsters were skipping along beside their father, chattering noisily.

Clark, too, seemed excited. Marty walked toward the door to meet the group.

"Good news!" he fairly shouted, taking hold of her waist and whirling both her and the baby around the kitchen. Marty held on tightly to Arnie, who was enjoying the whole thing immensely.

"'Sakes alive, Clark!" she said when she had caught her breath. "What's happened?"

Clark laughed and pulled her close. Young Arnie grabbed a handful of his father's shirt.

"Got great news," Clark said. "We got us a teacher."

"A teacher!"

"Yep—come fall thet there little school's goin' to be bustlin' with book learnin' and bell ringin'. Hear thet, Missie?" He stopped to lift the little girl up and swing her around.

"We got us a teacher," he repeated. "Come fall, ya can start off to school, jest like a grand lady."

"Grand ladies don't go off to school," Marty argued with a laugh. Then, nearly ready to explode with curiosity, she caught hold of her husband's arm. "Oh, Clark, do stop all the silliness and tell us all 'bout it. Oh, it's such wonderful news. Jest think, Missie, a teacher fer yer school. Ain't thet jest the best news? Who is it, Clark, an' where does she come from?"

"He—it's a he. Mr. Wilbur Whittle is his name, an' he comes from some fancy city back east—can't recall jest now which one—but he's jest full of learnin'. Been teachin' fer eight years already, but he wanted to see the West fer himself."

Missie came to life then. "Goodie! Goodie!" she shouted, clapping her hands, obviously just catching on to all the excitement. "I git to go to school. I'll read an' draw pictures an' everythin'."

"Me too," said Clare.

"Not you, Clare," Missie insisted in big-sister fashion. "Yer too little."

"Am not," Clare countered. "I'm 'most as big as you."

Marty wasn't sure where the argument would have ended had not Clark intervened.

"Hey," he said, sweeping up Clare, "ya'll sure 'nough go to school all right, but not yet. I need ya to help with the milkin' an' chorin' yet awhile. In a couple of years maybe I'll be able to spare ya when Arnie gits a little bigger an' can help his pa."

Clare was satisfied. Let Missie go to school. He'd sacrifice for a while. He was needed at home.

The commotion that the news stirred up was hard to control, but finally Marty placed Arnie in his chair with a piece of bread crust to chew on. Clare went with Clark to care for the horses and do the chores. Missie unbundled her kitten, explaining gravely that she would no longer be able to play as much. She was grown-up now and would be going off to school. Then she proceeded to lay out her best frock, clean stockings, and her Sunday boots—only about five and a half months prematurely.

Marty smiled at Missie's earnest preparations and went about the supper preparations with a song in her heart. This fall they would have their new school. Missie would get the long-coveted education. Would Nandry and Clae be as fortunate? Marty promised herself again that she would do all in her power to see it happen.

SIX

Wanda's New Baby

Warm April sun shone down on the earth, melting away the winter snow and bringing forth crocuses and dandelions. Marty rejoiced in the springtime sun, thinking ahead to the days spent planting her garden and tending her summer flowers.

The children, too, were delighted to now spend time outside in the sunshine. Clare tagged along with Clark whenever it was possible, and Missie enjoyed bundling up Little Arnie and taking him out to play. Clark had made a small wooden cart with wheels, and she carted the toddler all around the yard. When she—and Arnie—finally tired of that, she would return him to Marty and scamper outside to dig around in a protected area of soil near the house she had dubbed "my garden." Marty had given her a few seeds, and already some shoots of green showed where a turnip or some lettuce was making an appearance. Missie found it difficult to leave them alone and often was admonished for digging them up to see how they were doing. Her "garden" would have been much further along but for its periodic setbacks from its overly solicitous gardener.

Marty was about ready to ask Clark if he would turn the soil in the big garden for her, but then she cautioned herself not to get into too big a rush. The nights were still cool, and early plants might yet be damaged by frost. Still, she found it nearly as hard to be patient as Missie did.

In the meantime Marty put every available minute into knitting two baby shawls. One was for Wanda's new baby and one for Sally Anne's. Missie loved to watch the shawls take shape and begged to add a few stitches of her own. When Marty had to quietly undo the extra stitches, she set the child up with wool and needles for her own small project. Missie announced it would be a sweater for her kitty.

One evening as Marty sat waiting for the potatoes to boil for supper, using the time to add a few more stitches to the final shawl, Ole Bob started up with an awful racket outside. Marty had never heard him so fussed over something before. She looked out the window to see an approaching rider, and she understood why the dog was wrought up. Never had she seen such agitation and determination exhibited in a horseback rider. He was leaning well over the animal, using the end of the rein as a whip and pumping with his legs as though to produce more speed from the animal. The horse, already lathered, was breathing hard and obviously pushing forward with every muscle.

As the rider swung through the gate and straightened up, Marty could see it was Cameron Marshall.

Clark appeared from somewhere and caught a rein as the man threw them from him and slid to the ground. He could barely stand and supported himself on the rail fence. Marty's thoughts jumped to Wanda and immediate concern filled her. She rushed out of the house and met Clark and Cam coming in.

She looked to Clark with her unasked question, and he must have understood, answering her quickly to allay her fears. "Wanda's fine," he told her. "She is in labor, and Doc is there— but she is uneasy like, an' she wants you. I'll hitch the team, an' you can take Cam home. I'll bring his horse over later. The animal needs a rest now. She's already been to town an' back for the doc, an' now here."

Marty glanced at the foam-flecked, rather worn-out looking creature. So this was Cam Marshall's prize horse. She didn't look very promising at the moment, but maybe Clark would be able to coax some life back into her with feed and a good rubdown.

"I'll be right back with the team," Clark said, leading the limping, tired animal away.

"Come inside," Marty spoke to the man, who was still trying to catch his breath. "I'll jest take a minute to gather a few things."

He followed, though she wondered if he was really aware of his surroundings.

"Sit down there," Marty directed. She pushed the boiling potatoes toward the back of the stove. The meat in the oven was smelling delicious and made her feel hungry. At least supper would be ready for her family. She poured a cup of coffee and handed it to Cameron.

"Do ya take cream or sweetenin'?" she asked.

He shook his head.

"You drink this while I get me ready," Marty said, wondering if he actually was accustomed to drinking it black or just couldn't be bothered to think about it.

She left him sipping from the cup while she hurried to the bedroom and began to put a few things in a bag. She'd have to take Arnie with her in case the hours dragged past his feeding time. The other two tykes she'd leave in the care of their pa.

By the time she had put together what she needed and bundled up their small son, Clark was in the kitchen talking to Cameron. Marty noticed that Cam had downed the coffee. Maybe that would keep him on his feet at least.

Clark helped her to the wagon, where she deposited Arnie

into a small box filled with hay. They kept it in a corner of the wagon for the express purpose of bedding down the little ones. She then took her place on the seat, and Clark handed her the reins.

Cameron did not object to Marty driving the team. She was relieved, knowing instinctively that in Cam's present state of worry, Clark would be concerned about the team being pushed unnecessarily hard. Doc was already there, so Marty could drive sensibly. Even with this knowledge, though, she urged the team forward and kept them traveling at a fairly fast pace. Wanda had asked for her. She planned to be there as soon as she could.

By the time they reached the Marshalls' one-room cabin, Cameron had settled down and seemed again to be in control of himself.

He helped Marty from the wagon, handed Arnie to her, and placed her bag of belongings on the ground, promising to bring it in for her upon his return from settling the team.

Marty hurried into the house, placing Arnie on the floor on her coat while reminding herself to later see to having the box with its hay mattress brought from the wagon for him.

She crossed to the bed at the far end of the one room. Doc paid little heed to her approach, for Wanda was getting his full attention.

"May I talk to her?" Marty whispered.

"Go ahead," he answered. "Quiet her if you can."

Marty nodded. She found a place at the head of the bed and looked down at Wanda's pale face.

"I'm here," Marty told her friend softly.

Wanda tried for a smile. "You came," she said in a weak voice. "I'm so glad. I'm scared, Marty. What if—"

But Marty didn't let her finish. "Everythin' is goin' jest fine," she comforted. "Doc is here. Shouldn't be long now 'til ya have thet fine son—or pretty daughter—thet ya been want-in'. Jest ya take it easy an' listen careful to what Doc tells ya to do. He knows all 'bout birthin' babies."

Wanda looked unconvinced but said, "I'll try."

"Good! Now I'm gonna git yer man an' the doc some sup-per. 'Member, I'm right here iffen ya need me."

Wanda gave a slight nod, then closed her eyes again.

Marty squeezed her hand and left her to see what she could find to go along with the meat and loaf of bread she had brought for their supper. She was thankful that Arnie slept con-tentedly on. Cameron came in from the barn, but he seemed to want to stay as far as possible from his wife and the doctor at the other end of the room.

Supper was prepared, and Cam didn't even make the attempt to eat something. But Doc took a moment from his vigil to gulp a cup of coffee and eat a cold meat sandwich. Marty could read a bit of uncertainty in his face. It unnerved her and made her feel awkward and fumbling as she cleared the table and washed up the dishes.

The single room seemed overcrowded with people and anxiety. Cameron left to pace back and forth beneath the stars. Marty found a moment to whisper an inquiry to the doc.

"She should have delivered by now," he answered honestly. "I don't like it. The baby is small and sure doesn't need that added struggle to get into the world. I'm afraid the extra time will weaken it. I'm thinking of sending for Mrs. Graham. I hope I'm wrong, but I'm afraid that once that baby's here, it's going to take all we've got to keep it with us."

Marty prayed a silent prayer, the tears flooding her eyes.

"I'll send Cam," she whispered to the doctor.

She carefully removed all traces of her tears. There was no need to alarm Cameron further. She went out into the cool night and found him sitting, head in hands, on the chopping block.

"Cam," Marty said. He looked up rather frantically.

"Doc says he'd like to have Ma Graham here, jest as an extra pair of hands like, so's one can sorta look to Wanda an' the other care for the baby when it comes. Doctors like to work with assistants, an' me, I know nothin' 'bout deliverin' babies. Ya can take the team. Doc says there's lots of time." She tried to keep her tone as matter-of-fact as possible.

Cameron got to his feet, looking relieved there was something he could do.

Marty returned to the house and listened for the team to leave the yard.

Good, she thought, *he's drivin' sensibly,* as she went to feed Little Arnie.

When Cameron and Ma arrived, Ma was able to relieve the doctor while he had a cup of coffee and then took a stretch around the farmyard.

Marty made more coffee, consoled Wanda, and put Arnie down for the night. She looked at him tucked into his hay-filled box and envied him. There was no place for anyone else to lie down.

After a long night of waiting and just after the new day had poured its dawn over the eastern horizon, the new baby made his appearance. Marty had gone to the woodpile to replenish the fire, and upon her return she heard the weak cry of a newborn.

Wanda, too, heard the cry and a murmur came from her pale lips.

"It's a boy," the doctor announced in the triumphant tone a doctor uses on such occasions. But Marty carefully watched his face to read his expression. She saw him go over to Cameron, and though he kept his voice low, she heard him tell the father that the baby was not very strong, but he'd do all in his power to save him. Cam simply nodded dumbly and sank back down on his chair.

Doc nodded to Ma to take over with Wanda, and he carried the fragile bundle to the table.

Marty was instructed to push the table nearer the stove and spread the small blankets to receive the little one, and there, with his satchel opened beside him, the doc waged a battle for life that would last many hours.

Marty instinctively knew he was calling on every bit of his training and available medication to assist him in the fight against the Grim Reaper. He quietly told her later that twice he thought he'd surely lost, but somehow a spark of life was again coaxed into the tiny body.

And so it was that twenty-eight hours later, when Marty and the doctor left for their homes, Wanda still had her baby boy, and Cameron's eyes spoke volumes about his thankfulness and appreciation. He even promised Doc his horse in payment for his services.

Ma remained to spend some days with Wanda until she was able to be on her feet again. Cameron took a couple of blankets to the hayloft for himself and spread a feather tick on the cabin floor for Ma.

Cameron seemed to have recovered from the ordeal and was already making boasts about the boy his son would become and the great things they would accomplish together.

Marty returned home so weary she could hardly guide the horses. Good old Dan and Charlie, given their head, found their own way at their own pace. And Arnie cheerfully enjoyed the ride from his convenient perch in the box behind his mother.

Clark strode quickly over to welcome Marty when she drove into the yard, as did two excited children and a dog half wild with excitement. Marty felt herself fairly drop into Clark's arms.

"It's a boy," she murmured, "an' he's livin'. Doc says he should make it now."

Marty reached her bed with Little Arnie. She held him close as she nursed him. He had been such a good baby through the whole difficult time. She kissed his soft head and then sleep claimed her. She never heard Clark enter the bedroom a little later to find the contented baby playing with bare toes and jabbering to himself and the tired mother sound asleep.

SEVEN

Mrs. Larson

The month of April brought new life into the neighborhood, but sadly, it claimed life, as well. Word came to Clark and Marty on a rainy Wednesday afternoon that Mrs. Larson had quietly slipped away in her sleep.

Marty was deeply concerned over the fact that Clae had been the one to find her. It seemed like the poor girl should have been spared that much at least, but her father, Jedd Larson, had not been home at the time.

The funeral was to take place the following day. The women in the community carefully bathed and prepared the body for burial, and the neighbor men built the plain wooden box in which it was laid. Marty took one of her own dresses over for Tina Larson to rest in, and Mrs. Stern was able to spare a blanket to drape the inside of the coffin.

The continuing rain made the digging of the grave a miserable task, but all was in readiness by the appointed time.

At two in the afternoon the farm wagons slowly made their way to a sheltered corner of Jedd's land where a short service of committal was held. Clark and Ben Graham were in charge.

Marty's heart ached and she wept for the two young girls standing huddled together in the rain as they watched their only source of love and comfort lowered into the ground. After a whispered conference with Clark following the service, she plucked up her courage and dared to approach Jedd with a suggestion that the girls come home with her for a few days "until things are sorted out."

"Be no need," he informed her. "There's plenty at home to keep their minds an' hands busy."

Marty felt anger rise sharply within her and turned away quickly to keep from expressing it. She wouldn't forget her promise to Tina Larson and would plan and work as long as she could to fulfill it—yet how was it ever to be accomplished? School would be starting in the fall, and somehow those two girls must be there. She'd pray more, and she knew Clark would join her in the petition. God had mysterious ways of answering prayer, beyond a person's imagination.

Marty bit her lip to stop its quivering, wiped the tears mingling with the rain on her cheeks, and went to join Clark, who was waiting in the wagon.

———

The death of Mrs. Larson hung heavy on Marty's mind during the next days and weeks. She could not rid herself of a deep burden for the girls now left without a mother and saddled with a father who didn't know how to cope with life in the best of times. She knew the poor little things were facing a loss too big even for an adult.

She visited the girls several times in the days following the funeral, taking fresh baked goods, vegetables, and cold meat. Still her heart ached within her each time she thought about them. She decided that a visit to Ma Graham was what she needed. Ma could help her think this thing through and come up with something that would help her persuade the stubborn Jedd to allow the girls their rightful and needful education.

Marty had come to know the girls much better during the days of Mrs. Larson's illness. Nandry, the older of the two, was quiet and withdrawn. Marty feared that even now it might be too late to help Nandry come out of herself and her recent sorrow to develop into a young lady capable of self-expression and self-worth. Younger Clae was like a small flower that had been kept out of the sunshine. Given a chance, Marty felt confident that Clae could burst forth into full bloom. Gradually she had lost her shyness with Marty, and Marty noticed that even though she was the younger, Clae was the one who often took the lead in conversations.

Marty set her chin determinedly. Somehow she must get that promised chance for those girls. At breakfast she approached Clark with her plan.

"It bein' sech a fine day, I thought I'd give the young'uns some air an' pay a visit to Ma."

"Good idea," he responded immediately. "Ground's not dry enough fer seedin' today. Ya can take the team. I'm gonna spend me the day cleanin' more seed grain jest in case it dries enough to plant the lower field later this spring. I'll bring ya the team whenever yer ready."

"Should be all set in 'bout an hour's time," Marty answered. "It'll be right good to have a chat with Ma. She hasn't been home that long from tendin' to Wanda and her baby. I'll be able to hear all 'bout how thet new boy's doin'."

"An' . . ." Clark prompted, looking intently into her face.

"An' . . . I'll maybe give her a chance to talk 'bout thet comin' baby of Sally Anne's. 'Magine she's gittin' right uptight waitin' on thet one, it already bein' on the late side."

"An' . . ." Clark prompted again.

Marty looked at him. All right—so he knew neither of those reasons was the real purpose for her calling on Ma. She sighed. "I wanna talk to her 'bout the Larson girls," she answered forthrightly. "Clark, somethin's jest got to be done 'bout 'em, but I'm not smart enough to figure out what."

Clark pushed aside his empty porridge bowl and rose to get the coffeepot. He rested a hand on her shoulder as he poured Marty a second cup, then refilled his own and returned the pot to the stove.

So that's it, his eyes seemed to say, but he sipped the coffee silently.

Finally he spoke. "Jedd Larson be a mite bullheaded. Seems unless he decides thet his young'uns need thet edjecation, there's not much hope of anyone changin' his mind."

"I know thet," Marty mourned. "Oh, I wish I had me some way of persuadin' 'im. Do ya think you as a man talkin' to 'im might help?"

Clark shook his head. "Jedd never did listen much to my say-so."

"It's so selfish and mean," Marty stormed, "jest plain mean."

"Don't fergit thet those girls be gittin' his meals an' washin' his clothes."

"It's still not fair."

Clark's eyes twinkled. "Maybe ya'll have to pray the Lord to send along a new Mrs. Larson."

Marty didn't think it was funny. "I wouldn't pray thet on any woman—no matter how ill I thought of her," she shot back with eyes flashing.

Clark just smiled and rose to his feet. "Don't know of any other way out," he said. "I'll have the team waitin'. C'mon, Clare, let's go git the horses ready. You too, Arnie, c'mon with yer pa."

The boys both responded joyfully to the offer—Clare with a bound toward the door and Arnie holding up his arms to be carried.

Marty hastened to clear the table and do up the dishes. Missie decided it was her turn to wash and thus slowed down the procedure, but Marty knew it was worth the extra time to encourage the little girl's helpfulness.

When they drew up to the Graham home, Ma was obviously glad to see them. She hurried them into the house, where her children welcomed the Davis youngsters and took them off to play. Nellie volunteered to entertain young Arnie, and Marty accepted her offer gratefully.

Ma and Marty sat down to a cup of coffee, warm nut bread, and a long-awaited chat.

"How's thet new boy of Wanda's?" Marty wondered.

"Tiny—but he's a spunky little'un. He's got a lot of fight in 'im fer sure."

"What did they finally name 'im?" Marty smiled, remembering the long list of names from which Cam and Wanda were trying to choose.

"Everett Cameron DeWinton John."

"Quite a handle fer sech a small bundle."

"Seems so, but maybe someday he'll fit it."

"I'm so glad he's doin' fine," Marty said with feeling. "It would have crushed poor Wanda iffen she'd lost another baby."

Ma nodded solemnly.

"How's Sally Anne?"

"She's fine, but she sure is tired of waitin'." Ma shook her head. "Ya know how it can seem ferever. I called over to see her yesterday. Even got the cradle thet Jason made all laid with blankets, an' she's jest achin' to fill thet little bed up. Still, I don't think the time's settin' as heavy on her as on her ma. I never dreamed I'd ever git so flustered like over the comin' of a young'un."

"Are ya gonna deliver her?"

"Land sakes, no! We're gittin' the doc fer sure fer thet one. Funny thing—me havin' delivered so many young'uns in my time, but jest thinkin' on thet 'un makes me feel as skitterish as a yearlin' first time in harness. We's all set to send Tommie off fer Doc at the first warnin'. I'll sure be glad like when it's all over."

Marty nodded. She'd be glad, too. She wondered what it would be like to see one's own daughter about to give birth. Must be a mite scary—knowing the pain but unable to share or relieve it. She reckoned that when it was Missie's turn, she'd be even more nervous than Ma. She pushed the thought from her and changed the subject.

"Ma, I really came 'bout somethin' else. Ya know I promised Tina Larson I'd do all I could to see thet Nandry and Clae had a chance fer their schoolin'. An' Jedd—well, I jest fear he won't be 'llowin' no sech thing. In jest a few months now thet schoolhouse will be openin' its door, an' Jedd Larson declares thet no daughter of his be needin' it."

Marty looked at Ma, the helplessness weighing her down. "What we gonna do to make 'im change his mind?"

"Reckon there ain't much of anythin' thet will make Jedd Larson change his mind, lessen he wants to. Me, I wouldn't know even where to begin to work on thet man. He ain't got 'im much of a mind, but what he has got sure can stay put."

"Yeah." Marty sighed and played with her coffee cup. There didn't seem to be much hope for her to keep her promise. What could she do? She had prayed and prayed, but Jedd did not seem to be softening in the slightest toward the idea of schooling for his girls. But she wasn't giving up yet. Maybe somehow the Lord could open the mind of that stubborn man.

As she helped Ma gather up the dishes, an excited Jason arrived at the door.

"Ma," he called, rushing in without a knock or a howdy. "Sally Anne thinks it's time."

"Tom's in the field by the barn," Ma told him quickly, all in a flurry. "Send 'im fer Doc and you come back with me." She grabbed a bag from a corner, threw her shawl about her shoulders, and left the house almost on a run.

Marty realized that the bag in the corner had been all packed and ready to go just for this eventuality.

Tom left the yard on a galloping horse, and Ma and Jason left at a not much slower pace in his wagon.

Marty gathered up her small family and headed for home. She was sure all would go well for Sally Anne and her baby. Still, she found herself praying as she traveled.

Later that afternoon Tom arrived with the glad news that Sally Anne was safely delivered of a small daughter and that Grandma and Grandpa were holding up fine.

"Jest think," he said proudly, "I'm Uncle Tom now. Guess I'll have to go out an' git me a cabin."

Marty smiled.

"What ya mean?" Missie queried. "Can't ya live at home when yer an uncle?"

Tom winked at Marty. "Yeah," he said, "guess I can. Guess they won't kick me out jest 'cause I'm an uncle. 'Specially when I'm an uncle who does most of the chorin'. Won't need me thet cabin fer a while. Anyway, I'm not in the mood fer batchin'." He paused, then said rather sheepishly, "I'll wait 'til I git me a cook 'fore I go movin' into a cabin of my own."

Marty suddenly realized that young Tommie was indeed growing up, and perhaps his jesting about a cabin of his own had more serious meaning than he pretended. How quickly they grew up and changed, these young ones.

Her mind checked the girls of the neighborhood. Would any of them be just right for young Tom Graham, who had so endeared himself to her when he had cheerfully done Clark's chores and spent his evenings reading to the young Missie? Now he stood before her on the threshold of manhood. Marty hoped when the time came for him to take a bride, he would find one worthy of him.

Tom sat bouncing Arnie on his foot and went back to the subject of his new niece.

"They still haven't decided fer sure on her name. Sally Anne wants to call her Laura, but Jason be holdin' out fer Elizabeth. Seems he read 'im a story 'bout an Elizabeth an' always wanted a daughter by thet name. Then he insists thet she should have Sally or Anne in her name, too. Elizabeth Sally sounds kinda funny. Me, I'm a favorin' Elizabeth Anne. What ya think?"

"I like it," Marty assured him. "I think it's a right pretty name."

"Me too," Missie joined in, anxious to share her opinion and make her presence known to her beloved Tom.

"Thet should settle it, then," he said. "I'll jest tell Sally Anne thet Missie says it should be Elizabeth Anne, so Elizabeth Anne it must be."

Missie grinned and clapped her hands with glee.

Tom placed Little Arnie on the floor and prepared to take his leave.

"I best be gittin'. Nellie will be mad iffen I'm late fer supper, an' there's still the chorin' to do. Don't s'pose I'll git much help from 'ole Grandpa' tonight." He enjoyed his teasing, but he said it with love and respect in his voice.

Marty smiled. "Tell 'Grandpa' thet we send our love," she told him.

With a nod and a wave of his hand, he was off.

"I like 'im," Missie whispered. "I think when I grow up I'll marry Tommie."

"My land, child!" Marty exclaimed. "Yer not yet six an' talkin' of marryin'. Let's not rush things quite so much, if that's all right with you."

"I didn't mean *now*," Missie explained firmly. "I said when I grow up. First, I gotta go to school."

E I G H T

A Strange Answer

The garden produced its welcome crops, and the warm summer sun began to be almost too warm to bear. Marty was glad for the cool breezes that blew off the nearby hills, and she chose the early morning hours for any necessary weeding and preparing for the harvest to come. Missie loved sun-ripened tomatoes and would eat her fill right off the plants when they were ready to pick.

But like the spring, soon summer, too, would be gone, and fall would be upon them. With the fall would come preparations for school. Correspondence with Mr. Wilbur Whittle assured them he had not changed his mind and would be arriving in late August to acquaint himself with the people and the area and to prepare the schoolhouse for the commencement of classes.

Arrangements had been made for the unmarried Mr. Whittle to board at the Watleys, and Mrs. Watley had her two grown-up daughters polishing themselves as well as the family silver.

Missie was counting the days. Her whole life was now filled with thinking of the new school year. What she would wear, what she would learn, and who she would play with were all very important in her daily planning and in her regular reports to anyone who would listen.

Missie had two deep regrets. One was that Miss Puss would need to put in long days alone in her absence, and the second was that Tom Graham had declared himself to be too old to attend school with all the neighborhood youngsters. She'd miss Tommie. She wanted very much to have him there. She would be so proud to stand and recite a well-studied lesson if Tommie were listening. She would work extra hard at her reading and sums if he were there to observe her skills. But Tom was not to be there, and Missie, though still excited about the prospect of school, was definitely disappointed.

Marty, too, was disappointed—not over Tom but over the Larson girls. The school term was only a few weeks away, and there had been no change in Jedd Larson's attitude. Marty was about to conclude that her prayers had all been in vain.

At their usual pre-breakfast prayer time, Marty was mulling over these thoughts in her mind as Clark read the morning Scripture: "'Ask, an' it shall be given you; seek—'"

I been askin', Lord, an' nothin's been happenin', she admonished her Lord and immediately felt guilt and remorse.

I'm sorry, Father, she prayed silently. *I guess I'm 'bout the most faithless an' impatient child ya got. Help me to be content like an' to keep on havin' faith.*

Clark seemed to sense her mood and in his morning prayer included this petition: "An', Lord, ya know thet 'fore long now our school will be startin', an' ya know how Marty promised Mrs. Larson to try an' see thet the girls got their schoolin'. Only you can work in Jedd's heart to let her keep thet promise, Lord. We leave it to you to work out in yer own good way and time."

Marty was deeply grateful for Clark's understanding and silently thanked him for his caring. Maybe now God would be free to act. He often did when Clark prayed. She immediately reprimanded herself. True, Clark seemed blessed with answered prayers, but she was God's child, too. And the Bible said that God did not regard one of His children above the other. If Clark's prayers were answered more frequently, it was because Clark had a stronger faith. She determined to exercise her own faith more.

Later in the day Ole Bob announced an approaching team. To Marty's surprise, it was Jedd Larson. It had been some months since Jedd had been over, and Marty could not contain a surge of excitement that this visit might be an answer to prayer.

Clark met Jedd outside and Marty could see them talking in a neighborly fashion while Jedd tied the horses to the rail fence.

Marty quickly put on the coffeepot and cut pieces of gingerbread. *I wonder jest how he'll say it without havin' to back down none,* she wondered.

Jedd and Clark were soon in and seated, and Marty fairly held her breath waiting for Jedd to spill the good news. He'd brought news all right—news that made him grin from ear to ear—but hardly what Marty had been expecting.

"Sold me my farm yesterday."

Clark looked up in surprise.

"Ya did? Someone local?"

"Nope—new guy jest come in. He was with thet wagon train goin' through—had planned to go further west, but his missus took sick. Decided to stay on here. I showed 'im my farm, and he offered me cash—outright. Good price, too."

Jedd stopped and looked back and forth between them, no doubt waiting to let his good fortune take proper effect on his hearers. Then he went on. "The train's restin' fer a couple of days 'fore goin' on. I'm thinkin' o' takin' his spot with the train. Al'ays did want to see what was further on. Never can tell—might find me gold or sumpin'."

Marty finally drew a shaky breath.

"What 'bout the girls?" she asked, trying to keep her tone even.

She knew it was a foolish question. All hope now of keeping her promise seemed to be vanishing. If Jedd was moving away, there would be no chance of the girls ever getting any schooling.

Jedd answered, "What 'bout the girls? Wagon trainin' won't hurt 'em none. Do 'em good to see more o' the country."

"But . . . but they're so young. . . ." Marty stopped. Something within her warned her to be silent, but she suddenly felt sick to her stomach as all her hopes and prayers came crashing down about her.

Jedd looked at her evenly but said nothing. He then reached for another piece of gingerbread and went on as though Marty had never spoken.

"This new man—name's Zeke LaHaye. Seemed to like the looks of my land real good—paid me a first-rate price fer it. He's got 'im three young'uns—a near-growed girl an' two young boys."

"Thet right?" Clark responded. "Guess I should pay me a call on 'em. Might want to send his young'uns to school."

Jedd snorted. "Don't know why he'd do a fool thing like thet. Both of those boys are big enough to git some work out of. Must be around twelve an' eight, I'd say. An' thet daughter's almost of an age to take on a home of her own. I been thinkin' myself thet she might be right handy to have along goin' west."

His meaningful grin made Marty feel further sickened.

"I s'pose," Clark said slowly, "thet a young, good-lookin' buck like you be takin' another bride 'fore ya know it."

He winked at Jedd, and Marty felt anger rise against him. *What is he thinking of, Clark humoring the despicable man this way?* she thought hotly.

Clark looked thoughtful, then broke the silence. "Ya know, I'm thinkin' thet when it comes to marryin' agin, a young woman might think twice 'bout takin' on two near-growed girls. 'Course an older, more sensible-like woman might not mind. Ya could always do thet, ya know—take ya an older, settled one 'stead of some flighty, pretty young thing. Might not be as much fun, but . . ."

Clark fell silent, and it was obvious by the look on Jedd's face that he was thinking on the words.

"Ya could leave the girls here, I s'pose, so's they wouldn't slow ya down none, either in yer travel or any other way." Clark gave Jedd a playful jab with his elbow. Jedd grinned.

"Hadn't thought of thet," he deliberated, "but those new folk gonna move into my house—hafta have everythin' all cleared out tomorra. Don't s'pose they'd want the girls hangin' on."

"Thet's tough," said Clark and appeared to really be working on Jedd's problem. "Kinda puts a man at a disadvantage like, don't it?"

Jedd looked worried. Marty wished she could excuse herself and go be sick. Never had Clark made her so angry—or so puzzled. To sit there feeding the ego, the very worst impulses, of this—this disgusting person, and disposing of his two daughters as though they were unwanted baggage—she was so upset she feared any moment she might lose her temper with both of them.

Then Clark seemed to suddenly think of something.

"S'pose ya could put 'em up here fer a while," he said nonchalantly. "We do have us an extry bedroom. Might jest be able to make room."

So that's where he's goin' with all this. Marty's climbing temper began to recede. Clark was using Jedd's self-image as a male of desirable qualities to try to fight for the girls. He was offering to keep them—take them off the man's hands, so to speak. Marty wondered why she hadn't realized immediately what Clark was doing. She sent Clark a quick imploring glance to show him she now understood and for him to please, please continue.

Jedd rubbed his grizzly chin. "Thet right?"

"I think we could manage—'til ya got kinda settled like." Clark grinned and jabbed with his elbow again.

Jedd appeared to be thinking carefully.

"'Course," Clark continued, a somewhat doubtful note now in his voice, "Marty has the say of the house an' how crowded in she wants us. Sorta up to her, I guess."

Marty wanted to cry out, "Oh, please, please, Jedd," but instead she took her cue from Clark and even surprised herself at her casual, matter-of-fact voice.

"S'pose we could . . . fer a while . . . iffen it'll help ya out some."

"Might do," Jedd finally said. "Yeah, might do."

Marty didn't dare look up. The hot tears in her eyes threatened to run down her cheeks and into her coffee cup. She quickly left the table on the pretense of tending to the fire. When she had herself somewhat under control, she poured the men another cup of coffee and then went to the bedroom where she leaned against the window ledge and prayed for God to please forgive her lack of faith and to please help Clark in the battle in which he was presently engaged.

A few moments later Clark came in, gave her shoulder a quick squeeze, rummaged in a drawer, then was gone.

Marty heard the men leave the house, and she went into the sitting room a short time later to watch Jedd's team on its way out of the yard.

Marty heard Clark come into the house and walk over to stand behind her at the window. As Jedd's wagon disappeared over the hill, Clark gently turned Marty to face him. Her tear-filled eyes looked into his and she hardly dared voice the question.

"Did he—?"

"Did he agree? Yeah, he agreed."

Her tears started again.

"Oh, Clark, thank ya," she said when she was able to speak. "I never, ever thought thet I'd be able to have the girls right here." She wiped at her eyes and sniffed, and Clark pulled out his handkerchief. "Thank ya," she said again.

Her face buried in his man-sized handkerchief, she then sputtered, "At first I was so mad, you talkin' thet way to thet . . . thet conceited . . ." She floundered to a stop, knowing she should not voice the words she had been thinking.

She began over again. "I couldn't imagine why ya'd say sech things 'til . . .'til I began to see. An' he believed it all, didn't he? Believed thet a woman—a young woman—in her right mind would take to him."

She was getting angry again at the very thought of it all, so she decided to change the subject before she worked herself up.

"An' he said thet we could take the girls?" she asked.

"Yep."

"To keep?" She couldn't help the pleading in her voice.

"Well, he didn't exactly say fer how long, but I'll be one surprised farmer iffen Jedd Larson ever wants his girls back. He'll git hisself all tied up in this or thet, an' his girls won't enter much into his thinkin'."

Marty had a sudden question she knew she shouldn't ask, yet she felt she needed an answer.

"Ya didn't make 'im pay fer their keep, did ya?"

Clark grinned. "Well . . . not exactly," he said slowly.

"Meanin'?"

"Jedd said thet we could keep the girls iffen we gave 'im ten dollars apiece fer 'em."

Marty pulled back. "Well, I never!" she retorted. "I never thought I'd live to see the day thet one had to pay fer the privilege of feedin' an' clothin' another man's young'uns."

Clark pulled her back against him and smoothed the long brown hair. Maybe he thought by so doing he could smooth her overwrought nerves. But when he spoke there was humor in his voice. "Now, now," he said, as though to an angry child, "ya wanted yer prayers answered, didn't ya? Who are we to quibble as to how it's done?"

Marty relaxed in his arms. He was right, of course. She should be feeling thankfulness, not frustration.

"The girls will be here tomorrow," he continued. "It's gonna be strange fer us all at first an' will take some gittin' used to. Seems thet all of our energy should be goin' into makin' the adjustment of livin' one with the other."

He lifted her chin and looked into her eyes.

"You've got yerself a big job, Marty. Already ya have yer hands full with yer own young'uns. Addin' two more ain't gonna lessen yer load none. I hope ya ain't takin' on too much. Yer tender heart may jest break yer back, I'm thinkin'."

She shook her head. "He answered our prayer, Clark. Iffen He thinks this right, what we're doin', then He'll give the strength an' the wisdom thet we need, too, won't He?"

Clark nodded. "I reckon He will" was all he said.

NINE

Nandry an' Clae

As he had agreed, Jedd arrived the next day with the two girls. Their few belongings were carried in a box and deposited in the bedroom that would be theirs. Marty wondered if the parting would be difficult, particularly so soon after the loss of their mother. But she could not detect any show of emotion from either side.

Jedd was obviously anxious to be off. He had his possessions packed in his wagon, and with the money from the sale of the farm laying heavy in his pocket, he was hard-pressed to hold back, even for a cup of coffee. He did fill up on fresh bread and jam, however, and with the food barely swallowed announced that he must be on his way. He seemed to be fully recovered from his wife's death. He gave Marty and his two daughters a quick nod, which Marty supposed was to suffice for thank you, good-bye, and God bless you, and went out the door. He was full of the coming trip west and all the good fortune he was sure it would hold. Jedd always had regarded good fortune more highly than hard work.

Thus it was that with no further fanfare, Nandry and Clae were established as members of the Davis household.

Marty decided to give the girls a few days of "settlin' in" before establishing routine and expectations.

She looked at their sorry wardrobes and decided that a trip

to town would be necessary if they were to be suitably dressed for the soon-to-commence school.

Marty seldom went to town, sending instead a carefully prepared list with Clark, but she felt this time she should go herself. Clark would find the selecting of dress materials and other articles difficult and time consuming.

Marty had been saving egg-and-cream money over the months and felt that now was the time to dip into her savings. It wasn't fair to lay all the expenses on Clark. He'd already had to pay Jedd for the privilege of raising his daughters. Marty felt her hackles rise again at the mere thought.

Well, that was all past and done—so be it. From here on the two youngsters were hers to care for, and to the best of her ability and with God's help—and some from Clark, too—she planned to do it right.

Nandry seemed her usual withdrawn self, neither expecting nor finding life to be interesting. But Clae clearly was observing everything around her and even dared at times to delight in what she discovered.

Both girls were surprisingly helpful—for which Marty was grateful. Nandry preferred to spend time with young Arnie rather than the other members of the family. Marty did not mind, for help in keeping up with the adventuresome and often mischievous little boy was always welcomed.

Marty planned her journey to town for the following Saturday. She would go in with Clark and thus save an extra trip.

On Friday after breakfast was over, she called the girls to her. It was time, she decided, that they work a few things out.

They sat down silently, their hands nervously twisting in their laps. Marty smiled at them in an effort to relieve their tension.

"I thought thet it be time we have a chat," she began.

They did not move nor speak.

"Is yer room to yer likin'?"

Clae nodded enthusiastically and Nandry more quietly followed suit. The additional bedrooms Clark and their neighbors had put on the cabin really came in especially handy now that the two girls were with them. Marty had made sure the bed was soft with warm, nice-smelling blankets, and she had put colorful rag rugs over the floor, printed curtains with ruffles at the window, and two framed pictures on the wall. A neat row of pegs was on the wall behind the door and a wooden chest stood beneath the window. There was even a small bench with cushions all of its own.

Clae nodded again and said with a sparkle in her eyes, "I never knew anything could be so fine. . . ." But she stopped when her sister gave her a long look.

Marty continued to smile.

"I thought maybe we should be sortin' out our work," she said. "Missie washes the dishes two mornin's a week, an' she cleans her room—makes her bed and hangs up her clothes each day—an' she helps some with Arnie, too. Now then, what ya be thinkin' thet you'd like to be doin' fer yer share?"

No response, although it looked like Clae might have something in mind.

"I know ya already been makin' yer bed. Thet's good; an' ya do a nice job of it, too. But is there anythin' ya 'specially like to do? Better than other things, I mean."

Still no answer.

Marty felt stymied, and just when she was wondering whether to simply make assignments as she saw fit, assistance came from her own Missie, who had come over to join the proceedings.

"Mama says I wash dishes good," Missie announced from her place leaning against her mother, "but I'll share. Do ya want to wash dishes sometimes, Nandry?"

Nandry nodded.

"An' do you, too, Clae?"

Clae nodded.

"Well," said Missie, very grown-up, "then why don't we take turns?"

It was settled.

Missie added, "We all need to make our own beds, but Clare is too little yet to make his bed, an' Arnie can't make a bed at all! Ya have to git 'im up an' dress 'im every day. Who wants to make Clare's bed an' who wants to dress Arnie?"

"I'll care fer Arnie," Nandry was quick to say.

"Then I'll make Clare's bed," Clae said cheerfully.

"An' sometimes there's special jobs," went on Missie, "like gittin' more wood or hangin' out clothes or peelin' the vege'bles."

"I'd rather feed the chickens," Nandry said slowly. "An' gather eggs," she added as an afterthought.

"She likes chickens," Clae informed the group. "She was always wishin' thet she had some. Chickens an' babies—thet's what she likes."

"Fine," said Marty to Nandry, "you can feed the chickens and gather the eggs iffen ya like thet. What 'bout you, Clae? What else would you be likin'?"

Clae looked suddenly shy. Finally she blurted out, "I'd like to learn to make things." She looked carefully into Marty's face as if to determine if she was going to get into trouble for her request. Finding no resistance, she added, "Pretty dresses an' aprons an' knitted things."

"Stop it, Clae," Nandry scolded her. "Ya know ya can't do all thet. Ya'd wreck the machine fer sure."

So now it was out. Marty had noticed the younger girl eying her machine hungrily. So she wished to be creative. Well, she would be given instruction and opportunity.

"The machine doesn't break so easy," she said, carefully choosing her words. "Ya must both learn to sew, an' then you'll be able to make whatever ya want. Perhaps we could start on somethin' simple, an' then when ya practice a bit ya can do somethin' more fancy. I learned to sew when I was quite young, an' I've always been glad I did. Sewin' somethin' pretty always makes me feel good inside."

Clae's eyes shone with a mixture of delight and disbelief.

Marty said, "Now, tomorra you're goin' to have yer first big job. I'm goin' into town with my husband to buy the things you'll be needin' fer school, an' I will be leavin' ya here on yer own." She looked over the faces arrayed before her and secretly wondered if she would be brave enough to leave them when the time came, or would she bundle them all up and take them along. No, that would never do. Five youngsters underfoot and hanging on her skirts and begging for this or that while she tried to hurry through a great deal of shopping just wouldn't work at all. Besides, the girls really did need the opportunity to prove themselves. They were quite old enough to be caring for younger ones, and she must give them the chance to show it.

Her announcement caused no change of expression on the faces before her.

"Do ya think, Nandry, thet ya can care fer young Arnie an' help fix some dinner fer ya all?"

Nandry nodded her head in agreement.

"An', Clae, you an' Missie will need to help with the dishes an' the dinner an' keep an' eye on Clare. Can ya do thet?"

The two girls exchanged glances, then nodded vigorously. Missie was obviously very pleased to be included with the older girls in this responsibility.

"Good," said Marty, "then it's decided. Now, we have lots thet must be done today. First, I want ya all to slip off yer shoes so I can get a tracin' of yer feet fer new boots fer school."

Marty's face flushed as soon as she realized the two Larson girls were not wearing shoes.

"Our shoes are all worn out," Clae explained matter-of-factly. "They won't stay on no more."

Marty carefully traced and labeled the feet on her pieces of brown paper. She would cut them out later so they could be slipped into a shoe for fitting.

"Now then," she told the girls, "Clae an' Missie are to do up the dishes. Missie, you show Clae where the pans an' towels are kept. Nandry, you come with me an' I'll show ya how to be carin' fer the chickens. Then we'll gather an' clean the eggs so I can add 'em to the ones I've set aside to take to town."

"Can I bring Arnie?" Nandry asked, uncharacteristically animated. "He likes chickens, too."

Marty consented, knowing Arnie did love the chickens, though Marty was convinced that what he liked the most was their delightful squawking and flapping when he chased them around the pen.

They left the house together. The two younger girls were already at work on the dishes.

Maybe things would fall into place after all. The girls seemed almost eager to get to their new tasks. Marty breathed a relieved sigh and led the way to the grain bin, Nandry and Arnie in tow.

A Trip to Town

Marty still had some nagging misgivings the following morning as she tied on her bonnet and gathered the eggs, butter, and cream for the trip to town. Should she actually leave them all on their own, or should she at least take Arnie with her? No, she told herself, she needed to establish a sense of trust and responsibility with Nandry and Clae. After all, their father had made them shoulder grown-up responsibilities for years. She couldn't require that they go back to being treated as children. So she again went over all the instructions with them, and they assured her they understood and would abide by her wishes.

But it was with reluctant steps she left to join Clark in the wagon. She waved good-bye once more and put on a brave smile.

"Bring us some yummies," Clare called to her.

"An' some new hair ribbons fer school," added Missie.

"Thet girl," laughed Clark, "she thinks far too much 'bout how she looks."

Marty coaxed forth a smile.

"Clark," she said as they left the gate, "do ya think it's good to leave 'em like thet—with jest the girls an'—"

"Why not?" Clark interrupted. "They been cookin' an' cleanin' fer years already."

"But they haven't had young'uns to care fer."

"No, thet's right, but carin' fer young'uns seems to be the one thing thet pleasures Nandry."

"I noticed thet, too," Marty responded. "She really seems to enjoy Arnie. An' he likes her, too. Oh, I hope it will be all right, but I won't feel easy like until we git home agin. I sure hope this is a fast trip."

"Yer frettin' too much, I'm thinkin', but we'll try to hurry it a bit. Won't take me long to take care o' the things I be needin'. How 'bout you?"

"Shouldn't take long. I need school things fer the girls an' the usual groceries."

"Ya need money, then."

"I have my egg savin's."

"No need to spend all yer savin's on outfittin' the girls. I'm ready to share in the carin' of 'em."

Clark tucked the reins between his knees and pulled out his wallet. He extracted a couple of bills.

"Think this is enough?"

"Thet'll be fine," she answered. "I 'preciate it. It's gonna take a bit to git 'em off to school proper like. They really own nothin' now thet's fittin' to wear."

Clark nodded. "Well, we knew when we took 'em thet they'd cost somethin'. No problem there."

They drove into town to find the streets filled with commotion. A wagon train was getting ready to move on. Dogs barked, horses stomped, and children ran yelling through the street. Men argued prices and women scurried about, running to the store for a last-minute purchase or looking for children who had been told to stay put but hadn't. Marty shook her head and decided she had picked a poor day to come to town—surely her shopping would be slowed down considerably.

She entered McDonald's General Store with some trepidation. She always dreaded facing the proprietor's scrutinizing eyes and sharp tongue.

"I declare," Marty had said to Clark on one occasion, "thet woman's tongue has no sense of propriety."

Missie had overheard the word and latched on to it, henceforth declaring of all things—particularly to young Clare—"You've no sense of pa'piety," which seemed to mean, "Yer jest plain dumb."

Marty had decided after that she'd better guard her tongue more carefully in Missie's presence.

Marty now straightened her shoulders to help her brace up before opening the McDonalds' door. To her relief, Mrs. McDonald was busy with three women from the train. She glanced at Marty and opened her mouth to call out something, but must have changed her mind to give full attention to her customers. Marty smiled briefly and crossed to the bolts of dress goods. What relief to be left on her own for making the selections. Mentally she calculated as she lifted bolt after bolt. The new dresses had to be serviceable, but, oh, how she'd like to have them pretty, too, and the prettier material added the cost up so quickly. The dark blue would wear half of forever, but how would one ever make it look attractive for a young girl? The soft pink voile was beautiful but looked like you could sip tea through it without even changing the taste. Hardly appropriate for a farm girl.

Mrs. McDonald was now enjoying the bits of gossip the travelers could supply, prying rather transparently for the whys of their coming or going. Marty weighed her decisions with care. She picked neither the dark blue nor the pink. *No use takin' material thet'll wear too long,* she reasoned. *They'll outgrow it 'fore ya know it anyway. But ya never know—maybe Nandry's can go to Clae, then to Missie. . . .* Eventually she selected a length of medium blue, a pearly gray color that she would make up with white collar and cuffs, some warm brown, and a couple of prints, one with a green background and the other red. She then chose materials for underclothes, nighties, and bonnets and moved on to choose stockings, boots, and some heavier material for coats. Until the colder weather arrived the girls could get by with capes she could make out of material she already had on hand.

As she added bolt after bolt to the stack on the counter to be measured off, she realized what an enormous sewing job she had ahead of her. She was thankful she already had worked on Missie's school clothes.

Missie! She had asked for new hair ribbons. Marty moved quickly to choose some for Nandry and Clae, too.

Her shopping was going well, thanks to the wagon-train ladies keeping Mrs. McDonald busy. She laid the last dry goods items on the counter and rechecked her list. Even with the money that Clark had given her, most of her egg-and-cream money would go. Well, she couldn't help that. She had promised Tina Larson she would give the girls a chance, and she planned on doing just that.

She went on to her grocery list, placing items on the counter as she selected them. Before she had finished, Clark entered the store. His eyebrows moved up at the great heap on the counter, but he made no comment.

"Most done," Marty offered. "Did ya git the things ya be needin'?"

"All but a piece fer the plow. The smithie had to order it in, but I expected thet. Thet's why I sent now 'stead of waitin' fer later." He grinned in anticipation. "There be jest a chance thet it'll make it fer spring plowin'."

The other women gathered their bundles and left the store, and Mrs. McDonald scurried toward Clark and Marty.

"Well, well, how are the Davises?" she began but left no time for a reply. "I hear thet ya took on them two Larson girls." Her eyes dared them to deny it, at the same instant declaring them out of their minds for so doing.

She now waited just a moment, but neither Clark nor Marty commented.

"I have my purchases laid out here, Mrs. McDonald," Marty said evenly. "I believe thet's all I be needin' today."

Mrs. McDonald went to work adding up the groceries, but her snapping eyes promised Marty she wasn't finished with her yet. When the woman had the total figured, Clark stepped forward to pay that bill, then began gathering up the purchases.

"I'll take the groceries on out to the wagon," he informed Marty, "then be back to help with them other things."

"I can manage 'em," Marty assured him. "Jest wait in the wagon fer me. Where is the team?"

"Jest across the street."

"Fine. I'll be there quick like."

Marty walked to the door with him and opened it as he went out, both arms loaded. She picked up the box she had left by the entrance, placing it on the counter.

"My eggs, butter, and cream fer today. I'd like 'em to go toward these things, please," she said to Mrs. McDonald, motioning toward the stack on the counter.

When she had figured the worth of the farm produce, Marty began to push bolts of material forward, naming the yardage she desired from each one. In between snips of the scissors, Mrs. McDonald managed to pry for tidbits that Marty was sure she would later be able to pass on to her next customers.

"Jedd said ya was most keen on keepin' the girls."

Marty nodded.

"People here figurin' as to why. Some say thet with yer own three young'uns, ya figured to need the help pretty bad. I said,

'Now, Mrs. Davis wouldn't stoop to usin' mere children like,' but . . ." She stopped and shrugged her shoulders to indicate she could be wrong.

"'Seemed to me thet it makes more sense to keep 'em fer their board,' says I. 'Girls thet age ain't much fer workin', but with Jedd jinglin' all thet hard cash, no reason the Davises shouldn't git in on some of it.'"

Marty could feel her cheeks flushing with anger. How this woman could goad her!

"Anyway, I says to folks thet, knowin' ya like, I'm right sure Miz Davis won't overwork those two, an' a bit of good hard work might be the best thing fer 'em. Never did care much fer those two—real shifty eyes. Grow up useless like their pa. I'll bet ya won't git much work outta those two, but iffen ya got a fair cash exchange—"

Marty could take no more.

"Mrs. McDonald," she said, trying hard not to let her anger show through her words, though she knew she probably wasn't succeeding, "we took the girls 'cause their ma wanted 'em to have a chance, an' I made a promise 'fore she died. I aim to keep thet promise iffen I can—an' there was no money, Mrs. McDonald. Fact is, my husband paid Jedd Larson to be 'llowed to keep his daughters."

"I see . . ." But Mrs. McDonald quickly recovered. "Thet's what I wanted to know. Why didn't ya say so without all the fuss? Some people are so closed like with information."

Then she added, "Thet's jest what I been figurin'. Thought me thet folks were wrong in their speculatin'."

Mrs. McDonald had scored again. *Why does she always get what she wants from me?* Marty fumed. She had told no one else of her promise to Tina except Ma, and Ma guarded secrets carefully. Now the whole county would know, and the story would change as it was passed from mouth to mouth.

She fought for composure, paid for the purchases, and quickly gathered her parcels. They made quite a load, and she wished she had accepted Clark's offer to return to help her.

"All them fancy things ain't fer those girls, are they? Seems to me stuck way out there on yer farm, ya could jest as leave patch up their old things."

"The girls will be goin' to school come September." Marty said the words firmly. And she recognized just a trace of pride in her voice. Well, so be it. Before Mrs. McDonald could say anything further, Marty resolutely headed for the door with quick steps.

As she entered the street the commotion from the wagon train was even more intense. The teams were lined up now, ready to leave within a few minutes. Horses still stomped, dogs still barked, and children still yelled, but the bartering of the men was over and the final purchases of the women had been made. People stood in clusters by the wagons saying farewells and giving last-minute messages to be passed on to someone at the other end of the journey.

The third wagon back must be simply a passenger wagon, Marty decided, for a miscellaneous group of people seemed to be aboard it. The canvas, for the present, was down, and several plank seats had been placed across the wagon box. Most of the passengers appeared to be making a journey of short duration, perhaps to a nearby larger center, for they obviously traveled light. Maybe men on business or women going out to shop or visit. Some of them had young children with them, and their faces showed anticipation at the prospect of the trip.

In the midst of the clamor and excitement sat a white-faced, somber-eyed lady with three small children. One child cried, another clung to his mother fearfully, and the third and oldest, a boy, sat hollow cheeked and drawn, simply staring ahead silently.

"Thet's Miz Talbot from the other side of town," said a voice at Marty's shoulder, and she turned slightly to see that Mrs. McDonald had come out from the store, no doubt to get in on all the excitement. "Never should've come west," she stated. "Not made of the right stuff. She's leavin'. Goin' back." Her words were clipped and sounded rather biting.

Marty looked at the poor young woman and wished with all her heart she'd had a chance to speak with her.

Suddenly a young man pushed through the crowd almost at a run. The oldest child jumped to his feet, arms open wide, and shouted with delight. The woman looked alarmed. Marty could not hear the words, but she sensed the man was arguing and pleading for the woman to stay. However, the woman just set her lips tightly and shook her head. Finally she turned her back on him completely, her shoulders held stiff and stubborn.

The order of "move out" was given, and with a creak and a grind, the cumbersome wagons began to move forward. The man had to disentangle himself from the arms of the crying child and gently push him back into the wagon. The child screamed and shouted after him, and Marty thought for one terrifying moment that he was going to jump.

All his life he'll wish he'd left those two little arms around his neck and kept thet young boy with him, Marty mourned.

The wagon moved on past her. She could not see the woman's face, but she noticed her shoulders had lost their defiance and were now shaking convulsively.

Oh, you stubborn thing, Marty's heart cried, *come back—come back,* but the wagon moved on.

Marty turned to see the man, hands over his face, leaning against a hitching rail for support, the sobs wrenching his body.

A sickness filled her whole being. It was wrong, it was wicked, it was so cruel to tear a family apart like that.

"Good riddance, says I," said the voice beside her, and

Marty turned quickly away and stumbled across the street to the waiting wagon.

Clark placed her bundles in the wagon box and helped her up. Then the team, at his command, moved out of town.

They traveled some distance in silence. The warm summer sun shone down upon late flowers waving at the sides of the road, and birds dipped back and forth in the path of the team. Marty's anger and hurt had begun to subside, but her confused thoughts still fought to sort it all out.

Suddenly she felt her hand gripped tightly and looked up into Clark's probing eyes.

"So ya saw it, too, huh?" he questioned.

She nodded dumbly, her eyes filling with tears.

He squeezed her hand again.

"Oh, Clark," she said when she finally felt enough control to speak. "It was so wrong, so awful, an' . . . an' . . . it could have been *me,*" she finished in a rush of emotion.

"But it wasn't," he answered firmly. "It wasn't, an' some-how . . . somehow, I really don't think it ever could've been."

Marty looked up in surprise to meet his even gaze. Their unspoken communication assured her.

"No," she finally said with similar conviction, "no, maybe it never could've."

Clark was right for her—so right. Their love was strong and good. The good Lord had prepared them for each other—even when Marty didn't know Him and even had loathed the thought of staying on with Clark. Yes, their love had promise—enduring promise.

E L E V E N

Family and Teacher

Marty and Clark's return to the farm found everything in order, and Marty couldn't help but breathe a sigh of relief. Arnie was very glad to see his mother, but he quickly forgot she had been gone and went on with his play.

Besides her usual daily chores and the garden, Marty had only a few weeks to complete the sewing she planned to do for the Larson girls. Nandry seemed to accept the new items as inconsequential, but Clae's eyes took on a shine as they laid it all out and distributed the various things to each. Marty began her sewing lessons with Clae almost immediately and discovered her to be a good student. This pleased them both, and Clae soon was actually able to be a help and do more and more. Nandry also was shown how to sew, but though she went through the motions and did well enough at it, she never seemed to be too interested. She was much more involved in caring for Arnie and entertaining Clare. Nandry's contribution to the household was much appreciated. With the two small boys out from underfoot, Marty's and Clae's sewing progressed without too many interruptions, as did the other tasks that needed to be done.

Clark looked at the finished garments and smiled his approval. "My girls will all look jest fine a-sittin' in thet new schoolroom," he declared. Nandry flushed and Clae beamed at being included as one of "my girls."

Marty began to notice little things and wondered if indeed Nandry was a bit too taken with her benefactor. Clark's appearance was the only thing that ever brought a change of expression to Nandry's face, and Marty often caught her watching Clark as he went about the yard. She noticed as Nandry set the table that Clark's plate and cutlery were arranged with special care.

I think I'll be plum glad to git thet girl off to school, she thought with a sigh, then immediately reprimanded herself. *Ya silly goose,* she scolded inwardly, coloring in spite of herself. *Here ya are havin' jealous pangs over a mere child.*

It surprised her somewhat to discover this feeling. She had never been in a situation to feel threatened before, never having had to share Clark with anyone but her children.

"God, fergive me," she prayed, "an' help me not to be selfish with the man I love. Nandry is growin' up, perhaps too quickly, but it's by no choice of her own. She didn't have much to look up to in her own pa, an' now seein' a man, thoughtful an' carin', hardworkin' an' with humor in his eyes, no wonder she admires 'im like. Anyway, Lord, help me to be wise an' to be just. Help me to love Nandry an' to help her through these painful years of growin' up. Help Clark, too. Give 'im wisdom in his carin'."

Marty made no mention of her observations to Clark. There was no use drawing his attention to something of which he seemed to be completely unaware. It could accomplish no good and perhaps would only serve to put an unnatural restraint between the man and the girl, and Nandry so much needed to be able to reach out, to love and be loved. Secretly Marty hoped Clark would never realize the young girl was nursing a youthful infatuation.

For the most part, Clark was away in the fields, and though

Nandry took care of the chickens and the little ones in comparative silence, Marty observed her looking off in the direction that Clark was working and the flush on her face when he entered the house. Clark never did seem to notice and teased each of *his girls* equally.

Missie, being only "goin' on six," could still climb on her pa's knee, insist on combing his hair, or curl up beside him under the shelter of his arm.

Clare was his "helper" and followed his father wherever his young steps were able. It often meant a piggyback return, for the little boy played out quickly.

Arnie's toddler's steps determined to follow Pa, also, and Marty, looking out of the window, often shook her head at the patient Clark trying to complete his chores with two small boys "assisting" him, making his tasks most difficult. Yet she knew, all in all, Clark also found it enjoyable.

Though patient and loving with his family, Clark was very firm, and Marty at times had to bite her tongue when she felt Clark was expecting a bit too much for their tender years. She would have coddled them, but Clark would not, for he had a strong conviction that what was learned through discipline in early years would not have to be relearned through more painful lessons later on.

Clae seemed almost to have forgotten that she had ever lived elsewhere but with the Davises; and though neither of the girls called them Pa and Ma, Marty felt Clae truly looked on them as such. She openly admired Clark and enjoyed his teasing, even teasing back in return, her eyes sparkling with amusement.

So they adjusted to one another and began to feel like a family. Morning worship at the breakfast table was a special time. The two oldest girls listened carefully to things they had never heard before, while Missie and Clare coaxed for their favorite Bible stories.

Eventually enough of the sewing was done so the girls at least could start school dressed appropriately. Marty would finish the rest as she found the time.

Missie's excitement grew with each day that passed. Every morning she wanted to know how many days were left before school started. Marty felt the child was on the verge of hysteria and tried to slow her down. Clark just laughed and advised Marty to let Missie enjoy the anticipation. Daily, Missie changed her mind about what she would wear on her first day, going from plaid, to gray, to blue, to plaid again—over and over. Finally she settled on the blue because she liked her blue hair ribbons the best. Her only remaining sadness was that Tommie would not be there.

"I'm gonna marry Tommie," she informed Clae.

"Yer only five," Clae responded.

"Almost six, an' I'll grow," Missie retorted.

"But Tommie's 'most twenty."

"So!" said Missie with a mighty shrug of her shoulders, and that settled it.

It would indeed be good for Missie to have more contact with other children. Marty would be right glad when school was finally in session.

———

The Saturday before school was to begin was a day of high anticipation in the Davis household. The whole community was invited to a meeting at the schoolhouse, a chance for the parents and children to meet Mr. Wilbur Whittle and for him to be introduced to his pupils. Marty supposed there wasn't a home in the whole area that wasn't touched by the excitement.

The meeting was scheduled for two o'clock, and the neighborhood women had decided to serve coffee and cake at its closing. "Eatin' together always breaks the ice, so to speak," observed Mrs. Stern sagely.

At the Davis house the noon meal was a rather hurried affair, and the dishes were done in short order, in spite of Missie's constant chatter telling Clae all the things she was going to see and do come Monday morning. Marty gave careful attention to the grooming of each family member. Nandry and Clae had never looked better. Nandry still seemed rather non-committal about her upcoming chance at an education, though Marty did see her glance at Clark for his appraisal of her appearance. Clac, on the other hand, shone with excitement about this opportunity, running back and forth between Marty and the mirror to check on how she looked. With her flushed cheeks and the new ribbon tying back her hair, she looked downright pretty. The fact that Clae had helped to sew the dress she wore filled her with honest pride. Marty complimented her, making her rosy cheeks turn even brighter. Marty commented on Nandry's dress, as well, and the girl's eyes lit momentarily, but she didn't allow herself any further response.

Missie pranced around the house, singing and dancing. She had Clare and Little Arnie doing somersaults and jigs with her. Marty shook her head in exasperation as she tried to fasten a ribbon in her curls. Finally Clark and Marty were able to usher their brood out the door in some semblance of order.

It was a beautiful day for this welcome meeting of neighbors, and everyone seemed to have turned out for the important event. The wagons and teams were tethered at the far end of the school yard, with the folk gathered around outside and inside the schoolhouse, there not being enough room for them to all go in at once.

Neighbor greeted neighbor, with good-natured talk flowing all around. The two spring babies were there to be shown around and admired. Little Elizabeth Anne was radiant with smiles and coos. She insisted on being held upright so she wouldn't miss a thing, and even tried to sit on her own. A "bundle of wigglin' energy," her proud grandma Graham called her. Marty took a turn holding her and had to agree with the assessment, biased or not.

Wanda and Cam were there with their new son, Everett Cameron DeWinton John. Marty had thought it a rather long name for a small boy but was surprised to learn that his father, after all his grand ideas for his son, had cut it down to plain "Rett." Baby Rett had gained rapidly after his somewhat difficult birth. He was already a big boy for his age.

"Look at thet, huh," his father announced. "Look at thet fer a boy, an' 'im not yet five months. Gonna be a big fella, thet 'un." He grinned broadly, and Wanda smiled quietly beside him.

Marty agreed and took the baby. She held Rett for some time, walking around the yard with him. Finally she had to acknowledge the little warning signals that shivered up her arms and to her heart. The baby did not move as an infant should. When she raised him to her shoulder, there wasn't the proper lift of his head. *Something is wrong with this baby,* her heart cried. She looked at his beaming mother, his proud pa, and prayed that her eyes hadn't betrayed her thoughts, that she would be proved wrong. But she could not shake a heavy feeling from her heart.

At ten past two the Watley family wagon finally pulled in with the new teacher sitting in front beside Mr. Watley. All eyes were on the man. Marty wasn't sure what any of the neighbors might have expected, but she was nearly positive none had pictured the man before them. They were accustomed to seeing strong, muscular farmers out here on the frontier, and this gentleman looked somewhat out of place. Not only was he short but very slight of build. What he lacked in size he seemed to compensate for with an enormous mustache. Though carefully tended and waxed on the ends, it nearly hid the lower half of his face.

His vest was a bright plaid material, and he wore white spats, most unusual this far west. Marty had to quickly hush Missie's loud whisper about "What's he got on his feet?" A bowler hat topped his small head, and he often reached for it, dusting it and then replacing it again.

Marty was relieved to note his expression held both friendliness and curiosity.

Clark had been asked to get the meeting going, and he gave his welcome to Mr. Wilbur Whittle in most courteous fashion and introduced him by name to the audience. They responded with smiles and applause, even the folks listening from outside. Clark then announced the name of each neighborhood family, having them stand together so they could be properly introduced and recognized. Mr. Whittle nodded and smiled at them in turn.

After all had been presented, the new teacher was given the floor. Marty expected to hear a small voice to suit the small man, but she was surprised when a deep bass voice emerged.

Why, he must've practiced fer years to be able to do thet, she thought in amazement.

But Mr. Whittle's voice was not loud, and his audience had to listen carefully to hear his words. He expressed his pleasure at being selected to be the instructor in their school.

Ya were all we could git, Marty answered silently.

He told them he was charmed with the fine boarding place they had so thoughtfully provided.

She was the only one with room, Marty added mentally.

He was gratified to behold the fine facilities and careful selection of instructional aids.

Marty wasn't quite sure what he was referring to, so she let that comment pass.

He was looking forward to an amicable relationship with each one in the community, adult and child alike. He would look forward to making their further acquaintance, for he knew it would be both stimulating and intellectually rewarding.

Well, yes, sir! Marty felt like saying along with a salute, but of course she didn't.

Classes would begin on the following Monday at nine o'clock sharp, the bell employed at five minutes of the hour. Each child was to be seated and ready to commence the opening exercises on the hour. No tardiness would be accepted. Two recess breaks of fifteen minutes each would be given during the day, and an hour at midday to allow for the partaking of the noon meal and a time of physical stimulation for the students. Classes would end at three o'clock each day.

The children would get the benefit of his undivided attention and unsurpassed education, having been trained in one of the country's foremost institutions, recognized universally for its top-quality professors and its comprehensive and exhaustive courses.

He continued on in like vein for a few minutes more, but Marty's attention was diverted by Mrs. Vickers when she leaned toward Mrs. Stern and whispered rather loudly, "I hope he means he still is plannin' to teach."

Mrs. Stern vigorously nodded her assurance that he so intended.

The meeting finally ended with the community crowd giving the teacher a rousing round of applause, and he beamed on the group and withdrew.

Marty and the other women served the coffee and cake, and the animated visiting among the neighbors resumed. When she was finished, Clark sought out Marty to introduce her to the new neighbors on the Larson place.

The LaHayes seemed to be a nice couple. Mrs. LaHaye still looked thin and drawn but assured Marty she was feeling much better and was sure she'd soon be back to full strength. After an unspoken exchange between Marty and Clark, the LaHayes were invited to join the Davises for Sunday dinner the following day.

Mr. LaHaye said he was disappointed his journey west had been cut shorter than he had planned, but he was farmer enough to see the possibilities in Jedd Larson's good farmland. He had plans for building a new farmhouse and outbuildings, and he had already undertaken some much-needed repairs until he could replace them.

Tessie, their only daughter, was a bit plain but pleasant. Marty took to her immediately. Nathan, the older boy, appeared to feel smugly confident about his own wit and ability. The younger boy, Willie, had an endearing sparkle in his brown eyes. At the same time a hint of mischief alerted Marty there was no tellin' what this youngster would think to try next.

"How old are ya, Willie?" Marty asked.

"Nine," he responded good-naturedly. "I been in school before. Took three grades already."

Marty wondered if he thought that put him in a class by himself, for it was a well-known fact that none of the children in the area had as yet had any formal education.

"Guess ya'll be able to help the other young'uns here quite a bit, then," Marty said and watched carefully for Willie's reaction.

"Some of 'em," he said nonchalantly. "If I want to. Some . . ." He hesitated. "I might help *her*," he said with a grin, pointing a finger.

Marty followed the direction he pointed and noted with a

bit of alarm that the "her" on the other end was none other than Missie.

"Don't expect she'll need more help than the teacher can give," Marty said firmly. "She's startin' first grade, an' she already knows her letters and numbers."

Willie shrugged again and continued to grin. "Might help her anyway," he said. Then he was off on a run to join the other children.

The LaHayes were leaving early. He had much to do, he told the Davises. Shouldn't really have taken the time off, but his wife fussed about gettin' the boys in school. Well, they'd better git on home. He had a pasture to fence to supply his cattle with better grazin'. Glad to make acquaintance. They'd look forward to Sunday dinner. He shouted for his brood—and then they were gone.

School Days

Instead of being bright and sunny as had been ordered, Monday dawned overcast and showery. Missie couldn't hold back a wail of despair as she looked out of the window.

"My new blue dress will get all wet," she cried. "An' so will my brand-new hair ribbons."

Clark came to the rescue by offering to hitch up the team to drive the girls to school. This idea met with unanimous approval, and Missie's cheerful disposition returned even if the sun did not.

Marty carefully packed lunches and supervised the combing of hair and cleaning of fingernails. She wasn't sure who was most excited, but it no doubt was a close race between Missie and herself.

Clark decided that Clare and Arnie could go along for the ride in spite of the drizzly day.

"They won't melt," he assured Marty, "an' it will be good fer 'em to feel a part of the action."

The breakfast prayer that morning included the three new scholars—that they would study well, show their teacher respect, and use what they would learn for the bettering of self and everyone they would meet, now and in the future.

After the meal was over, the excited group left the house, and Clark covered the girls in the wagon to keep the rain off their new clothes. Clare and Arnie, feeling proud and important, took their places beside Clark on the wagon seat. Marty felt a tightness in her throat as she watched the eager faces, taking particular note of Missie's shining eyes. And then they were off.

"First school, then courtin' and marriage, an' gone fer good," she said softly. " 'Fore we know it, they'll all be gone—one by one."

She blinked her eyes quickly and turned back to the dishes. Soon Clark would return with Clare and Arnie, and all the work of their care and nurture would fall on her now that the girls were away much of each day. She must hurry through her tasks to be ready to spend much of this rainy day indoors amusing two restless little boys.

When Clark brought the boys back to the house, Marty changed them into dry clothes and made suggestions as to what they might like to do. She had thought she was prepared for what was in store but found it was even more difficult than she had imagined.

Arnie fussed and refused to be distracted with toys. Clare whined and pouted, insisting that he should be able to go to school, too. When he failed to convince his mother, he plagued her to let him go out to play. She pointed out the window at the wet landscape, but Clare only complained the more, seeming to imply that Marty could do something about the weather if she would just put her mind to it.

Marty finally gave them each a cookie. Arnie shared his with Miss Puss, then immediately undid all his generosity by deliberately pulling the kitten's tail. She responded with a well-deserved scratch to his hand. Arnie's howls brought Clare on the run. He chased the cat behind the kitchen stove and proceeded to poke at her with the broom handle. Marty sent Clare to sit on a chair while she washed the scratches on Arnie's hand.

By midmorning the clouds cleared away and the sun returned. Marty was glad to send Clare outside. She imagined him staying out only long enough to get thoroughly wet, but even that would give her some measure of respite.

As she suspected, the puddles drew Clare like a bee to flowers, but he played in them only long enough to become soaked and muddy. He stood at the door grumping that there was nothing to do. Marty despaired as she cleaned him up. Whatever would she do with them through this long, long day? And what if it rained tomorrow. . . ?

With noon's arrival Clark came in for lunch. The boys squealed with delight, and Marty breathed a sigh of relief. He could talk and play with them for a bit, and after the meal she could tuck them in for a nap.

But the usual naptime didn't go well, either. Arnie fussed and fretted, trying to climb out of his crib, and Clare never did go to sleep. So then they were cranky when she finally got them up.

The seemingly endless day finally righted itself when the three girls came home. Arnie ran to Nandry with a glad cry, and Clare began a list of questions for Missie to see if she really had learned anything. Clae stood by smiling demurely.

Marty had to raise her voice to be heard above all the chattering. "How'd it go?" she asked.

"Oh, Mama," cried Missie, "it's jest so great! Guess what I learned—jest guess. Here, I'll show ya."

"I want to see," Marty told her, "an' I can hardly wait. But first how 'bout ya all change yer school dresses an' hang 'em up nice." The girls quickly went to comply, anxious to be able to tell their news.

The time until supper was spent telling of the day's many activities. Only Nandry had nothing to offer. Missie jabbered on about the teacher, the other kids, the new work, her desk, and the poor fire in the potbellied stove.

"Know what? I don't think Mr. Whittle ever built a fire

b'fore. From now on, Silas Stern is gonna build it. It smoked somethin' awful."

She stopped a moment to pet the cat. "I like Mary Lou Coffins. She's my favorite friend—'cept fer Faith Graham."

The Coffins were new to the area, Marty knew.

Missie continued, a twinkle in her eye. "Guess what?" she said in a whisper. "Nathan LaHaye likes Clae."

Clae blushed and protested but not too vociferously.

"He does, too," declared Missie. "He pulled her braids an' everythin'."

Marty had no idea what the "everythin'" might be.

Then Missie's expression took on fire. "But I hate thet Willie LaHaye. He's a show-off."

"Missie—shame on ya," admonished Marty. "We are not to hate anyone."

"Bet God didn't know 'bout Willie LaHaye when He made thet rule," Missie declared. "*Nobody* could love him."

"What did he do thet was so terrible?"

"He reads—he reads real loud, an' he reads everythin'—even the *eighth primer*. He thinks he's smart. An' he teases, too. He said thet I'm too cute to be dumb. He said he'd help me. I said, 'No, you won't,' an' he jest laughed an' said, 'Wait an' see.' Boy, he thinks he's smart. I wish Tommie was in school with me."

Missie tossed her head in a grown-up fashion, and Marty wondered where her little girl was, so suddenly replaced by this rather dismissive young lady.

Please, prayed Marty, *don't let school change her thet much—thet fast.* But the next moment the little girl was back again.

"Can I lick thet dish, Mama? I got so hungry today, an' guess what, Mama? Mary Lou has a shiny red pail to carry her lunch in. Could I have one, too, Mama? It has a handle on it to carry it by, and the letters on it are white."

"What kinda pail is it?"

"I don't know yet. I don't know the words, but it's so pretty, isn't it, Clae?"

Clae agreed that it was.

"Could I git one, Mama, please?" begged Missie.

"I don't know, dear—we'll have to see."

"I don't like carryin' my lunch in thet old thing," pouted Missie. "Mary Lou's is lots nicer."

"We'll see" was as far as Marty would go.

The subject of school was dropped for the moment, but Missie picked it up again after supper when she had her father's attention.

"An' Mary Lou has a shiny red pail fer her lunch—with white letters an' a handle. Can I have one, too, Pa, please?"

"Are shiny red lunch pails necessary fer learnin'?" Clark asked.

"Not fer learnin'—fer lookin' nice," Missie answered, her voice determined.

At least she's honest, thought Marty wryly.

"We'll see," said her pa.

"Thet's what Mama said," Missie objected.

"Ya have a wise mama," Clark told her with a grin.

Missie wrinkled her nose but said no more, no doubt figuring she'd best not press it further—for the moment.

———

The days fell into a routine. Gradually the two little boys accepted the fact of the girls' absence and adjusted their play to include each other.

The girls settled into a pattern of learning. Missie, quick and eager, was soon leading her class, even without the help of Willie LaHaye, she was proud to note to her mother. Clae, too, had taken to school and surprised and delighted both the teacher and the Davises with her ability. She loved books and would have spent all her time with her nose buried in one or another of them had she been allowed to do so. Only Nandry seemed to drag her feet each morning at the thought of another day spent in school. Marty noticed it and wished there was some way she could help the girl. She knew most of the beginners in the school were much younger than Nandry and this in itself would be a discouragement to her. Marty endeavored to encourage without nagging at her.

Missie was the little busybody who furnished the household with all the news. One day she came home giggling, and Clae joined in.

"Guess what?" Missie announced. "When Mr. Whittle wants to yell loud, his voice goes from way down deep to a funny squeak." Missie demonstrated as she said the words.

Marty hid her smile, attempting to support an attitude of teacher respect.

"The big boys like to make 'im yell so it happens," Missie continued. "It sounds so funny, Mama, an' then he gits real red like an' growls real low—like this." Missie's six-year-old growl was rather comical.

"I hope ya don't laugh at yer teacher," Marty cautioned as solemnly as she could.

Missie looked sheepish, but then she raised her head to say, "Bet you'd laugh, too, but I jest laughed a little bit."

Missie also had frequent reports on "thet Willie LaHaye."

Willie LaHaye had dipped her hair ribbon in an inkwell.

Willie LaHaye had chased her with a dead mouse.

Willie LaHaye had put a grasshopper in her lunch box.

An' Willie LaHaye had carved her initials with his on a tree by the crik an' she'd scratched 'em out.

An' furthermore, she hated thet Willie LaHaye, an' she bet God didn't even care.

Thet dumb ole Willie LaHaye.

THIRTEEN

Somethin' New

When Clark made his next Saturday trip to town, Marty was glad there was no good reason for her to go along. She might have enjoyed the outing, being sure now that the girls were quite capable of watching over the others while she was gone. But going to town meant having to meet up with Mrs. McDonald. The woman never failed to get Marty in an emotional corner. Marty declared she'd rather face a bear or an Indian.

Actually, Marty had come across very few Indians since she had come west. Those she had seen or met in town or along the road seemed friendly enough. Most of the Indians in their area had moved on up into the hill country or had settled on a reserve set apart for them. Some wondered how they managed to survive, but most of the community told each other "an Indian is an Indian," and the prevailing opinion was that Indians were able to survive on very little. As long as the Indians were no threat to their well-being, the settlers were content to let them ride the hills hunting for meat and tanning necessary hides. On the other hand, they felt neither responsibility for nor obligation to the welfare of the Indians in the area. Marty was a bit uncomfortable with the general attitude but didn't quite know what to do about it.

As for the bear—Marty was glad she had never had reason

to concern herself with one of those. Like the Indian, the animals were content to remain in their native hills, away from the smell and the guns of the settlers. Occasionally a neighbor lad felt he must venture into the hills and return with a bearskin to place on the cabin floor or hang above the fireplace. This was a symbol of the conquering hunter rather than a necessity.

Even when gazing at a huge fur hide in a neighboring home, the head still carrying the fierce beady eyes and the long yellow teeth, Marty was sure the bear was preferable to facing Mrs. McDonald. So Marty avoided town when she could, somewhat ashamed of herself for doing so, yet content in her weakness.

Since school had begun, Marty always looked forward to Saturdays. It gave her a chance to catch up on many extra jobs because the girls kept the little boys out from under her feet.

And this time she had particular tasks because tomorrow would be a special Sunday. The new schoolteacher was coming to share the Sunday dinner with them. Marty was both anticipating the visit and dismayed by it. What was this odd-looking man really like? Missie brought home both positive and negative reports—one moment praising him, the next critical of some unusual conduct, and the next breaking into uncontrollable giggles over what she considered silly deportment.

Marty had set her freshly baked pies on the shelf to cool and was carefully cleaning two young roosters when Clark drove into the yard.

As usual, his return brought the children running to meet him. Marty, watching from the window, saw Clark climb slowly and carefully down from the wagon. At first Marty was concerned, wondering if Clark had somehow been injured or was not feeling well, but he straightened up and walked normally as he headed for the house, the youngsters in tow. Marty noticed that he carried something inside his jacket—there was a bulge there and he seemed to be carefully guarding it as he walked. The children had spied it, too, and they clamored to see what he was carrying, but Clark just grinned and motioned them on to the house.

Now, what's he up to? mused Marty, shaking her head as she watched the little parade come in the door.

"What is it, Pa?"

"Whatcha got, huh?"

"Show us, Pa!"

Clark finally pulled back his jacket, and a tawny curly head poked out. Sharp little eyes blinked at the sudden light, and the commotion around him brought a joyful wiggle to the little body. Shrieks filled the air, and each of the children pleaded to be the first to hold the little cocker spaniel.

"We start with the littlest first," said Clark, handing the squirming bundle to Arnie. Arnie giggled as he held the puppy close. It was the first time Arnie ever had a face-wash from a puppy's warm tongue. He laughed out loud.

Little boys and puppies belong together, thought Marty. Arnie must have thought so, too, for he was most reluctant to pass the puppy on to Clare.

As the children enthused over the new pup, Marty found opportunity to speak to Clark.

"Where'd ya git 'im?"

"The smithie's dog had a litter. Jest big enough now to wean. This one looks like the pick o' the pack to me."

"Sure is a bright one."

"Yeah, an' look at the eyes, the head—looks like a smart 'un."

The children finally agreed to put the puppy down so they could watch it waddle and prance across the kitchen floor.

"Look at 'im! Look at 'im!" they cried, giggling and clapping at his silly antics.

"Well," said Clark, "let's take 'im out an' see what Ole Bob thinks of 'im."

Ole Bob was truly becoming *old*. His legs were stiff and unaccommodating, his eyes were getting dim and his movements slow. Clark and Marty had realized that Bob's days were numbered, but perhaps with care, he could be with them for a while yet.

The family followed Clare carrying the puppy out to the doghouse. Bob came out slowly, stretching his stiff muscles, and wagged a greeting to them all.

As the puppy was placed on the ground, Bob lowered his head slowly and sniffed. He didn't seem impressed, but he wasn't put off by the new arrival, either. The puppy, upon catching sight of one of his kind, went wild with excitement, bouncing and bobbing around on unsteady feet like a funny wind-up toy whose spring would not run down. Ole Bob put up with this ridiculous display for a few moments, then walked away and lay down. The puppy toddled after him and began to tug at his long, fluffy tail. Bob chose to ignore him as the children shrieked their delight.

Eventually the puppy was left with Ole Bob. Clark and the boys went to put away the team and unload the wagon. The girls, after filling the puppy's little tummy with warm milk, returned to the chores they had been assigned. The family needed to decide on a name for the new dog. This would be discussed and settled at the supper table.

Marty went in to finish washing the chickens and wipe off the cupboard top so Clark and the boys could place the groceries there for her to put away.

As she went through the bags and boxes, she suddenly stopped, a pail marked LARD hanging from her hand. "What's this?" she asked. "I didn't have lard on my list, did I? And you got three pails of it. I got lard stacked up high from our last butcherin'."

Perplexed, Marty picked up her list and glanced over it to see what she might have ordered that Clark had read as "lard."

"No," he answered evenly, "ya didn't have lard on the list."

"Then why. . . ?" Marty left the question hanging.

Clark was looking a mite sheepish. "They're red, ain't they—an' shiny—an' they have a handle—an' white letters?"

Then it dawned. *Missie's pail. Red and shiny with white letters—LARD.*

"Now, I ain't sayin' thet Missie should have thet jest 'cause she asked fer it," Clark hurried to explain. "No reason fer her to be thinkin' thet she'll always git what she's wantin' jest by askin', but iffen ya think it won't hurt none fer her to have it— like this once, then it'll be there. An'—well, I could hardly git her one an' not the other two—now, could I?"

"No, I s'pose not."

Clark turned to leave the kitchen. "Ya can decide," he said again as he left.

Marty turned back to the three red, shiny pails. Three pails of lard, and she already with more lard than they could use, and another fall butchering coming up soon. What would she ever do with it all?

"Ya ole softy," she murmured, but she was forced to swallow over the lump in her throat. The thought of the happy faces and Missie's glowing eyes when she passed them their lunches on Monday morning made it difficult to wait.

The chores had been done and the Saturday-night bathwater put on the stove to heat in the big copper boiler when the family gathered around for the evening meal.

"I thought iffen somethin' happens to Ole Bob, it'll make

it less painful like iffen they have a new pup to fill their minds," Clark confided in Marty as she dished up the potatoes. She nodded.

Clark moved on to the table and saw to the seating of his family.

"Know what, Ma?" said Clare. "I stopped to see the puppy, an' it's all curled up sleepin' with Ole Bob. Does Ole Bob think he's the puppy's mama?"

Marty smiled. "No, I doubt Ole Bob is thet dumb, but as long as the puppy doesn't torment 'im too much chewin' an' chasin', Ole Bob'll be content to let 'im share his bed."

"He's so nice," enthused Missie. "I wish he could share my bed."

"Oh no," said Marty firmly. "Animals belong outside, not in."

"Miss Puss—" Missie began. Marty's eyebrows went up as she waited for Missie to confess that the kitty occasionally did climb into bed with her. But Missie must have thought better of it.

"Well," said Clark, "thought of any good names yet?"

"I think we should call 'im Cougar," said Clare.

"Cougar, fer a dog?" Missie sounded unimpressed.

"Thet's the color he is," argued Clare.

"I like King or Prince or somethin' like thet," said Missie.

"Fer a little puppy?" Clare was just as incredulous.

"He'll grow," Missie said defiantly.

"What about you, sport?" Clark asked Arnie. Arnie pushed in a big spoonful of potatoes and gravy with the help of his free hand. He shifted them around, swallowed some of the bite, and then answered, "Ole Bob."

"But what ya want to call the new puppy?"

"Ole Bob."

"But Ole Bob is the name of—Ole Bob," Clark finished lamely.

"I know," said Arnie. "I like it."

"Ya want Ole Bob an' Ole Bob," repeated Clare, obviously thinking only he was really capable of understanding and interpreting young Arnie's desires.

"Yeah," said Arnie, nodding his head. "Now we got . . ." Two rather potatoey fingers struggled to stand upright with the rest remaining tucked in. "Now we got two Ole Bobs."

The family laughed, but they all finally agreed that the new puppy would carry the name of Ole Bob, as well.

"He'll grow," said Missie sagely.

"Yeah, an' he'll git old someday, too," said Clare. " 'Sides, when we call 'em, we'll jest hafta say one name an' they'll both come."

Clark smiled. "Save ourselves a heap o' time and trouble thet way, won't we?"

Arnie grinned. "Now we gots a little Ole Bob an' a big Ole Bob."

As it happened, big Ole Bob did not remain with them for long. As Clark had hoped, the loss of the old dog was much easier for the children to accept with the growing young pup running and nipping at their heels.

Tommie's Friend

Before it seemed possible, the school year was coming to a close and it was time for the summer break. Some of the older boys had left school early in order to help with spring planting. The rest stayed in class until June. Missie celebrated completion of first grade by bringing home bouquets of flowers and red ripe strawberries in the beloved red pail that had, over the winter months, lost a little of its shine.

Summer was full of work in the garden and enjoyment of its produce. Marty often looked around her as she and the children gathered its bounty and thanked the Lord for His blessings. Missie, Clae, and Nandry now used their pails when picking beans and corn and tomatoes. And summer, of course, was expecially busy for Clark as he and neighbors helped one another with their harvests.

Then it was fall again, with the excitement of school preparations. Poor Clare was still a year short of school age and grumbled about having to "stay home with the little kids." Marty wasn't exactly sure who all he was referring to, since there was just Arnie, but at least he didn't complain about it for very long.

Clae and Missie both were anxious to return to class. Clae had spent the summer poring over books that Mr. Whittle had supplied and was closing the gap to where she should have been. Mr. Whittle was pleased and told her so.

Missie delighted in learning, and she loved to read to Arnie and Clare whenever she could get them to sit still for a bit.

Only Nandry remained out of sorts about the whole idea of schooling. She didn't say much on the subject until school opening was just days away.

"I'm not goin' back," she declared, her tone boding no argument, "—not with all those little kids."

Clark and Marty discussed it privately and finally decided that, as much as they were reluctant to do so, they would allow her to drop out.

"We'll jest have to concentrate on the homemaking an' the baby carin'," said Marty. "Nandry has the makin's of a good wife an' mother. Maybe thet's plenty. An' at least now she can read and write some. And I can work more with her on the schoolin' here at home."

Clark nodded in agreement. At fifteen, Nandry seemed quite capable of caring for a home. Some area young man was bound to welcome her eventually as his helpmate.

It was easier this time to watch Missie heading out the door that Monday morning. And actually it was easier to manage the boys because Nandry was there to provide supervision. Marty was very pleased to see the rather withdrawn young girl beginning to blossom in an atmosphere of love and nurture.

Marty also welcomed Nandry's extra pair of hands because of the fact that in only two months the Davis family would increase again. With little direction, Nandry assumed the lion's share of the youngsters' care, taking them with her to feed the chickens, putting Arnie down for his naps—Clare having declared himself too big for such "baby stuff"—and in general assisting with the household duties. Marty greatly appreciated her help and often told her so.

Marty was sitting in the coolness of the cabin with a pile of mending one afternoon when she heard an approaching horse. She laid aside the sock she was darning and went to the window.

"Why, it's Tommie," she said over her shoulder to Nandry, who was rolling out a piecrust. "I wonder what's bringin' him out our way." She moved quickly to the door.

"Tommie," Marty called to him, "do come in. We haven't seen ya fer jest ages."

He came into the kitchen and nodded toward Nandry, who flushed and dropped her eyes back to her work.

"How're yer folks?" Marty wanted to know.

"Fine, we all are fine. Thet little Lizzie be growin' like a weed."

"Isn't she a sweetheart?" Marty said. The last time she had seen little Elizabeth Anne, she was practicing her newly learned skill of walking. The tottering steps were awarded with lots of praise, hugs, and kisses by doting grandparents and her young aunts and uncles.

Marty recalled with a pang that little Rett Marshall still was unable to sit properly alone. She took a long breath and turned her attention back to Tommie. "I hear ya got yer own land."

"Yep," he said proudly. "Even got a small cabin on it. Not very big, but it should make do fer a while."

"Farmed it yet?"

"Nope. I take over come spring."

Could young Tom be showing interest in their Nandry? Her thoughts were interrupted by Tom's voice.

"Mind taking a little turn outside? It's a first-rate day an' kind of a shame to waste it."

Marty quickly determined he was talking to her, not Nandry, and she reached for her shawl.

"Be glad to," she said. "Been wantin' to take a little look at the spring afore freeze-up. Nandry, you'll keep an eye on the boys?"

At the girl's quick nod, Marty led the way outside. Their conversation as they walked continued with news of weather, crops, and family. They reached the spring, and Tom sat down on the cool grass, his back against a tree trunk. Marty watched him, realizing from his expression that something was bothering him. Still Tom said nothing. She watched him pick up a piece of bark and break it with his fingers.

"It's 'bout a girl, right?"

He looked up quickly. "How'd ya know?" he asked.

"It shows," Marty said with a smile.

"Yeah, guess maybe it does."

He waited a moment, then said, "She's special, Marty . . . really wonderful. I . . . I had to talk to someone. Ma wouldn't understand . . . I'm sure she wouldn't."

Marty was perplexed. What did he mean?

"Maybe yer selling yer ma short," she wondered.

"No, I don't think so. Iffen she'd give herself a chance to git to know her . . . then she'd understand. But I'm afraid at first . . . thet's why I came to you, Marty. Ya know Ma. Could ya . . . could ya talk to her like, an'. . . ?"

"Is she . . . is the girl from around here?"

"Not really. She's . . . she's from back in the hills. She lives there with her grandfather."

"An' her name?"

"It's Owahteeka."

"O-wah-tee-ka . . . why, thet sounds like an—" Marty broke off her sentence as she realized what Tommie was telling her. "She's . . . she's an Indian girl," she finished quietly.

Tom just nodded.

"Yes, Tommie, I see," Marty finally said. Looking at the

anguished face of the young man, she did not know what else to say.

She walked away a few steps as she tried to get things to fall into some perspective, but somehow she couldn't think through her muddled thoughts and emotions.

Dear Father, she prayed silently but fervently, *please help us work this out.*

When she returned to Tom, she chose a stump near him and lowered herself onto it.

"All right," she said, "I would like to hear about her. Where did you meet Owahteeka?" she asked, saying the unfamiliar name carefully.

Tom took a deep breath. "I met her last fall," he began. "The first time I saw her I was out looking fer a couple o' stray cows. They'd crawled the fence and gone off into the hill country, an' I went after 'em on horseback. I didn't find 'em thet day, but on my way home I found this here saskatoon patch, great big juicy ones, an' I stopped an' et a few. An' then I decided to take some to Ma fer a pie, so I took off my hat an' started fillin' it with berries.

"While I was pickin' I suddenly could feel eyes lookin' at me, an' I looked up, half expectin' to see a black bear or a cougar, an' there stood this girl—her eyes and her hair were black as a crow's wing. She was dressed in buckskin with beads, but what really hit me, she was laughin' at me. Oh, she was tryin' not to, but she was, all the same. Her eyes jest . . . jest lit up like, an' she hid her mouth behind her hand.

"When I asked her what was so funny, she understood my English an' said she'd never seen a brave pickin' berries like a squaw afore. Thet made me kinda mad, an' I told her maybe her braves weren't smart 'nough to know how good a saskatoon pie tasted.

"She stopped laughin' an' I cooled off some. We talked a

bit. She told me her name—Owahteeka, meanin' Little Flower. Either way, it sounded pretty.

"Well, anyways, we met agin—many times. In the winter months I used to leave her venison or other game. She lives alone with her elderly grandfather. He couldn't stand the government reserve so moved back alone to the hills. Owahteeka jest shakes her head when I ask if I can go to her home ta meet 'im. He's old—very old. Actually, he is her great-grandfather, an' when he's gone, she won't have nary a person left. She says she'll go back to the reserve—thet someone will take her in or some brave will make her his wife. But I don't want thet."

He looked directly at Marty now. "Marty, I want to marry her. I love her. I . . ." He groaned. "How am I gonna tell Pa and Ma?"

Marty shook her head. Poor Tommie. Poor Ma. And what would Ben. . . ?

Marty stood up and pulled her shawl about her, feeling a sudden chill in the air.

"Oh, Tommie!" she said, shaking her head. "I don't know . . . I jest don't know."

Tommie, too, got to his feet.

"But ya'll talk to 'em? You'll try—won't ya, Marty?"

"I'll try," she promised. "But Tommie, ya know . . . ya know it's not gonna be easy . . . not fer yer folks . . . not fer her grandfather, either."

"I know." He swallowed hard. "I know, but I've thought it all out. I've got my own land, my own cabin. It isn't much, but she's lived the winter in a tent of skins. A cabin should seem good after thet. We won't have to mix much with folks. Our land is sort of off by itself like. We won't bother no one. She'll be close to the hill country—she loves the hills. And she can see her people some—"

"Yer not thinkin' ahead, Tommie," Marty interrupted. "Yer

not thinkin' straight. Babies—family—what about that? Ya can't jest hide the young'uns away from yer families. Think about yer ma—how much she loves you, how much she loves her grandbabies."

Tommie's face dropped into his hands. "Thet's the only answer I don't have," he said, his voice so low she could hardly hear the words. "The only one. But . . . we'll . . . we'll work thet out when the time comes," he said, lifting his face to look into hers.

Marty didn't know what to say.

"Please, Marty," Tom begged. "Please try to talk to Ma. Iffen Ma can see it, she'll convince Pa. Please . . ."

Marty sighed. "I'll try," she promised, but tears filled her eyes. "I'll honestly try, but I'm not sure how good I'll be at it."

Tommie stepped forward and gave her an impulsive hug.

"Thanks, Marty," he whispered. "Thet's all I ask. An' . . . an' . . . someday I'll take ya with me to meet Owahteeka. When you see her, you'll know why . . . why I feel like I do. Now I gotta run."

He turned to go.

"God, please bless Tommie," Marty whispered as she watched him walk away. "And Owahteeka. . . ."

FIFTEEN

Search for a Preacher

A meeting of the community was called for on a Saturday afternoon in early October after the fall harvesting had been completed. All the neighbors were invited to attend and very few declined the opportunity to get together once again.

Zeke LaHaye sent word that though the meeting no doubt was a worthwhile one, he was hard put to keep up with his farm work and just couldn't spare the time.

The neighbors already had discovered Zeke LaHaye could spare no time from his farming duties—not to honor the Lord's Day, not to help a neighbor, not for any reason. Clark, who rarely made comment on a neighbor's conduct, confided to Marty, "Thet poor farm sure must be confused like—first owner Jebb Larson contents himself to let everythin' stay at rest; next owner nigh drives everythin' to death. Makes me stop short like an' look within. I hope I never git so land hungry and money crazy thet I have no time fer God, family, or friends."

Marty silently nodded a fervent agreement.

They gathered at the schoolhouse on the specified Saturday. Ben Graham would be in charge of the meeting. When the noise of visiting had subsided to a lull, he rose to his feet.

"Friends and neighbors," Ben began, "I'm sure ya all know why this meeting has been called. Fer some time now our area has been without a parson. Twice a year we've had the good fortune of a visitin' preacher passin' through our neighborhood an' stoppin' long enough to preach us a sermon and marry our young men and women.

"We're concerned thet this ain't enough to give our young'uns the proper-like trainin' in the truths of Scripture. And us older folk need to be taught the Word of the Lord, too, and reminded what's important in life.

"A few of us met a while back and talked it over, an' we feel it's time to take some action. We has us a schoolhouse now. This here fine buildin' is a tribute to what we can do when we work together. Now's the time fer us to go to work together agin."

Some people began to applaud and others cheered. Ben seemed somewhat flustered by it all, but he soon recovered, cleared his throat, and went on.

"What we need to do at this point is to choose us two or three men to form a committee to look into the gittin' of a preacher. One thet will stay right here fer regular-like services, fer the buryin' an' the marryin' anytime of the year. For the preachin' of the Word."

Again people applauded. Ben looked to Ma for support. He must have been encouraged by what he saw in her expression, for he raised his hand for silence in order to continue.

"We're gonna take names now as to who ya would like on the committee. It can be two men—or three iffen ya like. Any more then thet makes it a bit cumbersome."

A man near the back stood and called for Clark Davis to be on the committee. Marty heard several ayes for the nominee.

Todd Stern named Ben Graham, and again people voiced approval and heads nodded.

Mr. Coffins then stood and in a loud voice announced Mr. Wilbur Whittle for the committee. Awkward silence followed.

Marty guessed no one in the room knew what particular religious bent the new teacher might have. Finally feet began to shuffle, throats to clear.

Ben stepped forward. "Ya all have heard Mr. Coffins's choice. Mr. Whittle, are ya willin' to let yer name stand to help in the selectin' of a new preacher?"

Mr. Whittle rose to his feet rather grandly. "I believe I have many connections in the East that could indeed be of great assistance to the men on the committee," he offered in his carefully modulated voice.

"An' yer willin' to serve?" asked Ben.

"Certainly, certainly," agreed Mr. Whittle. "I believe that a resident minister will be a great asset in our community."

"Thank ya, Mr. Whittle." Ben looked around at the group. "Ya all have heard the three names given: Clark Davis, myself, and Mr. Whittle. What is yer pleasure?"

"So let it be," called a voice from the back of the room.

"We will vote," declared Ben. "Those in favor say aye, those agin, nay." There were no nays.

After the meeting, Mr. Whittle sought out Clark and Ben, nodding courteously to Ma Graham and Marty as they chatted nearby.

"Now, gentlemen," he began rather formally, "I am personally acquainted with many seminarians whom I have no doubt could fill our need quite adequately. Do you wish me to act as correspondent on behalf of the committee?"

Ben looked uncertain, but Clark answered, "I reckon you could do the letter writin' iffen ya wish. First, though, we'd like to know a bit 'bout these here fellas you'll be writin' to."

"Most certainly," said Mr. Whittle. "I shall draw up a résumé of each candidate for presentation, and you can select the ones whom you would want me to contact."

"This, ah, re-su-may," said Ben, "would thet be like an acquaintantship?"

"Acquaintantship?" inquired Mr. Whittle. Then, nodding rather vigorously, "Precisely—precisely."

"You go ahead an' do thet, Mr. Whittle," said Clark, "an' then Ben and me will go over thet list with ya."

"Fine, gentlemen, fine," said Mr. Whittle and strutted away looking quite pleased with himself.

————

The new teacher had heard so much back east about westerners not letting the easterner into the inner circle to become part of their frontier life. Yet here he was, out only a year and now serving on an important committee—a very important committee. After his contribution here, his place would be secure, he was sure.

He would go to his rooming house where he stayed at the Watleys, to his bedroom, close the door, and comb his memory for the best possible candidates he could recall. Scholars—he knew lots of scholars and some who would even be willing, just as he himself had been, to venture west to sample the excitement of opening a new frontier.

The West had its drawbacks, he was willing to admit, but there were compensations. One of them, in his case, being Miss Tessie LaHaye. Back east the young ladies had the less-than-cordial habit of turning away when they saw him approaching. Tessie entertained no such coyness. True, she was barely eighteen and he thirty-two, but in the West people seemed to quibble less over such social niceties. He was willing to accept her as a very pleasant young lady, and she seemed equally willing to accept him as an eligible man. In fact, he felt that she was rather impressed with his bowler hat and white spats. He planned to make a call on Miss Tessie—he hoped very soon, for he was anxious to discover just where he stood. And this meeting and his membership on the committee to find a preacher had given him the added confidence he needed. He no doubt would have to tread carefully, since Mrs. Watley clearly had her eye on him for her oldest daughter, but he surely would keep himself out of that quagmire, he assured himself as he sat down at his desk to begin his list.

SIXTEEN

Marty Talks to Ma

Marty put off the visit to see Ma as long as she could, but eventually she knew she must make the difficult call. Tommie was counting on her, and she had given her promise. Soon winter with its cold and snow again would make such a trip much more difficult to manage, and then she would be exhausted physically as well as emotionally.

What can I use as a reason to call on Ma? she asked herself but could come up with nothing. Finally she just decided to go.

Clark was heading for town for his usual Saturday trip, so Marty said, "Thought I'd trail along iffen it not be upsettin' anythin'."

He looked pleased. "My pleasure," he said. "Isn't often enough I git to show off my wife in town."

"Oh, I'll not be goin' on into town," she quickly told him. "I'm plannin' on stoppin' off to chat with Ma while ya be doin' yer errands."

His smile of pleasure faded a bit but not altogether. "Well, at least I'll have me yer company fer a spell," he said.

Marty informed the girls of her plans. Nandry seemed more than content to be in charge of the children and have the place to herself.

Marty put on her coat and tied on her bonnet. Her coat wouldn't button properly over her expanding waistline, so she had to be content with just pulling it about her.

Clark eyed her as she struggled up into the wagon, clumsy in spite of his helping hands.

"Ya sure this be the proper time to be takin' a bumpy wagon ride?" he asked.

"Won't hurt me none," Marty assured him.

She did notice that he drove more slowly than usual.

Ma's surprise at opening the door to Marty was quickly replaced by pleasure.

"I'm so glad ya came whilst ya still could," she said. Marty was relieved that Ma assumed her reason for coming was simply a social call and that this would be her last opportunity for a while.

They talked of this and that over cups of coffee, both women doing handwork as they chatted. Marty kept one eye on the clock, knowing she mustn't put her purpose for coming off too long. Finally she took a deep breath and began, "Tommie came to see me a while back."

Ma looked up, no doubt more at the tone of Marty's voice than the words themselves.

"He needed to talk," Marty explained.

Silence.

"A girl, huh?"

"Yeah. Ya knew about her?"

"I thought as much—it shows, ya know. He's got all the signs, but I can't figure it. He ain't said nothin' at all 'bout her. I've tried to lead in thet direction a few times, but he shies away."

Silence again.

"Somethin' not right about it? Is thet it, Marty?"

Marty swallowed hard. "No, not thet, really. Jest . . . well, jest different . . . yeah, different."

"Different how?"

Marty nearly choked as she took another swallow of her coffee to delay the inevitable. "Well, this here girl thet Tommie loves . . ." She paused a moment, then rushed on, "An' he truly does love her, Ma . . . I saw thet by the way he talked . . . the way he looked. Well, this here girl . . . her name is . . . is Owahteeka."

Marty looked quickly at Ma, and she could tell immediately that she caught the significance. Her needles ceased clicking, her face looked pale, and her eyes held pain.

"Tommie?" she whispered.

"Yeah, well . . . ya see . . ." Marty now felt the need to hurry with an explanation. "Tommie wasn't lookin' for this to happen. Ya see, he was jest lookin' fer stray cows, out in the hill country, an' he stopped at a berry patch to pick some berries fer pie. An' . . . an' this girl was there, too, pickin' berries, an' they started talkin' . . . she does speak English . . . an' then they got to know each other better over the months like. An' . . . well . . . Tommie loves her. An' it sounds like she loves Tommie."

Ma laid aside her knitting and rose to her feet.

"But he can't, Marty, they can't. Don't ya see thet? It jest doesn't work. It always means sadness, sorrows—always."

"I see," Marty said slowly, "but Tommie doesn't."

"What did he say? Don't the girl's people care?"

"She doesn't have people—thet is, no one but an old man—a grandfather. They haven't told 'im yet. Owahteeka thinks . . . thinks it better to wait," Marty finished lamely.

"To wait, huh?" repeated Ma. "Then thet'll stop 'im from doin' somethin' foolish. Maybe there's somethin' more thet we'll know then?"

"I don't know," said Marty, trying to carefully feel her way along. "The way Tommie talked, I don't think the grandfather will be around long. An' . . . an' . . . I don't think she plans to tell him. Jest wait 'til he's gone—an' then go ahead. Thet's what I think," she finished in a rush.

"Oh, dear God," Ma prayed, nearly weeping, "whatever are we gonna do?"

Marty sighed and leaned back in her chair. Who was she to try to give advice to a woman like Ma Graham?

"Well, seems to me," she finally said, weighing every word, "ya have only a couple choices. Ya can fight it an' probably lose Tommie, or ya can come to terms with it and welcome an Indian daughter-in-law."

Marty tried to read Ma's expression as she paced the floor between the table and the stove. Suddenly Ma stopped and straightened her shoulders.

"Marty," she said, "I jest thought me of a third choice. I won't fight it an' I won't encourage it, but I sure am goin' to do some prayin'."

"Prayin'? How?"

"Prayin'—how do ya think?" The words tumbled out from Ma. "It jest won't work, Marty. An' I won't have my Tom hurt. Grandchildren thet ain 't anybody's grandchildren 'cause they're neither white nor brown. It ain't to happen, Marty."

"Iffen ya pray like thet, Ma," Marty spoke quietly, slowly, "will ya be askin' fer help? For both of 'em? Or jest givin' orders?"

Ma's shoulders slumped and tears slid down her cheeks. She did not bother to wipe them away. Finally the battle within her seemed to subside. She sat down heavily in the chair across from Marty.

"Yer right—course ya are. I'd like to pray thet God would jest quickly put an end to all this. It scares me, Marty. Truly, it does. I jest feel thet no good can come out of it—no matter what. I'll pray—I'll pray lots, an' I'll try hard to say, 'Thy will be done' an' truly mean it. But I'll tell ya now, Marty, it don't seem ta me thet God's wantin' folks of different races to be marryin' an' raisin' young'uns thet turn out ta not belong nowhere. God ain't fer bringin' confusion of ideas or skins, far as I can tell—nor hurt an' pain of bein' shut out, put down. How can thet be of Him, Marty?"

Ma didn't seem to expect an answer and stopped her discourse. She sat rubbing her work-worn hands together in agitation.

"Me an' Ben gotta have a long talk on this," she finally said. "Then the two of us will try an' talk some sense into Tommie. He's a good boy, Marty, and he's got a good head on his shoulders. He'll realize thet this can't be good—won't be good for him or for her, either."

She wished that Ma had left just a wee small crack in the door instead of closing it so firmly, but Marty only nodded. She felt she had not done what she had come to accomplish, had nearly promised Tommie she would do. Maybe Ma was right. Who was she, Marty, to know the proper way to handle such a situation? And surely as Ma spent time in prayer, if she were wrong it would be revealed to her. But it might take time.

Poor Tommie. Marty's heart ached for him. Somehow she felt that no matter how things went, there was heartache in store for the boy. If only there were some way to spare him the sorrow. She hoped Clark was well on his way back from town. She was feeling like it would be awkward for both Ma and her if she stayed much longer for this visit. And she was anxious to lay it all out for him on the quiet ride home.

SEVENTEEN

A Call on Wanda

Marty was busy at the kitchen table making Clark's favorite dessert. Clare came in from outside, pulled up a stool, and stood on it to watch her work.

"Are ya mad at Pa?" came his voice at her elbow.

Marty stopped rolling the dough and looked at the boy. "Whatcha meanin'?"

"Thet's his favorite," explained Clare. "Ya always make his favorite when ya been mad."

He jumped down and was gone before Marty could even answer. He had laid the words out very matter-of-factly, as though they bore no consequence and needed no explaining. Marty frowned. It was a while before the rolling pin again went to work on the dough.

Do I really do thet? she asked herself. *An' iffen I do, does it show thet much?*

The fact was, she hadn't had a fuss with Clark at all. She was simply softening him up a bit to ask him for the team so she could pay an afternoon call on Wanda. Certainly Clark was not one to keep his woman restricted to home, but he did have some rather stubborn notions when it was nearing her confinement time. Marty easily could envision Clark wanting her to stay put for the present. Maybe his favorite dessert would put him in a more pliable mood, she had reasoned, and then this smart young Clare had come along. If he could see through her so easily, it was quite likely Clark would, too.

Marty shrugged and couldn't help but smile wryly as she put the dessert in the oven. Her menfolk maybe knew her just a bit too well. It possibly was foolish to think of venturing out right now, but she really felt she should have a talk with Wanda.

Gradually the news was making its way from neighbor to neighbor that something seemed to be wrong with the Marshall child, and Marty held her breath lest word of the rumors get back to Cam and Wanda. She knew there was not much she could do, but she hoped she could just learn if Wanda was aware that her small son was—different. Marty felt that Wanda's acceptance of the fact would be her own protective wall—the only thing that could shield her from the hurt if the neighbors' questions and comments did get back to her.

The dessert baked to perfection, and Clark must have picked up the aroma even before he stepped through the kitchen door.

"Umm," he called ahead, "apple turnovers. Makes a man's mouth water."

Marty smiled but still felt unsure about how she should proceed with her request. Nandry led Arnie in and washed him up at the hand basin, and they joined the rest of the family at the table.

The meal was pleasant but a bit on the rushed side. Clark had pressing work to which he wanted to return as soon as possible. Marty knew she must not waste a moment before getting down to business.

"Ya be needin' the team this afternoon?" she began.

Clark gave her a long look. "Ya plannin' on pickin' rocks?"

Marty felt warmth rise into her cheeks, but she bit back a quick retort and instead spoke quietly, her voice controlled. "I thought as how I'd like to take me a quick trip to see Wanda."

"It could be a mite quicker than you'd planned for."

Marty got his implication with no difficulty.

"Oh, Clark," she said with some impatience, "I been through this before. Now, don't ya think if my time was close I'd be knowin' it?"

Clark looked unconvinced. "As *sudden* travail cometh upon a woman," he said, looking at her with meaning in his gaze.

Marty was sure she had lost the argument.

Clark finished his coffee in silence and rose to go.

"Tell ya what," he said, stopping as he put on his coat, "iffen yer so set on seein' Wanda, I'll drive ya on over."

"But yer work—"

"It'll keep."

"But it's not at all necessary," Marty told him. "I'll be jest fine on my own. Honest, Clark, there's no need—"

"It's my drivin' ya or not at all—take yer pick," Clark said, his voice telling her the discussion was over.

Marty swallowed a lump of anger. *Yer so stubborn. Most as bad as Jedd Larson,* she shot back, though silently.

"All right," she said finally, her anger still churning her insides. "I'd be much obliged iffen ya'd drive me over."

"I'll be ready in fifteen minutes," Clark said and went for the team.

Marty turned to the table and vented some of her anger on the dirty dishes.

"Ya gonna make another apple dessert, Ma?" asked Clare.

Marty felt like swatting him.

"An' you, boy," she said instead, "you go out an' haul in some firewood. Fill up the woodbox—right to the top—an' be quick 'bout it, too."

Clare went. Marty knew she had been unfair. Clare was used to hauling wood, and goodness knew it wouldn't hurt him any, but she hadn't needed to take out her frustrations on him.

The ride to the Marshalls' was a fairly silent one. Marty still felt peevish, and Clark did not make any attempt to draw her out. When they arrived, Clark went on to the barn, where Cam was working on harnesses, and Marty went in to see Wanda. Little Rett lay on the floor on a blanket.

Wanda's eyes shone as she spoke of him. "He can sit up real good now," she told Marty and went over to demonstrate.

But, Wanda, Marty wanted to protest, *he's a year and a half old. He should be walkin'—no, runnin'. He should be runnin' after his pa and sayin' words. And here you are gloryin' in the fact that he can finally sit.*

But of course Marty did not say it. She merely smiled her approval at Rett's achievement as he teetered back and forth, trying to maintain a sitting position with his mother catching him when he was about to topple over. Wanda talked on enthusiastically, and soon the men joined them.

They were seated at the crowded little table when Marty felt the first labor pain. It caught her by surprise, and she stiffened and tried to breathe slowly and regularly. She soon felt normal again and hoped no one had noticed the episode. When the next one came a few minutes later, she felt Clark's eyes upon her and looked up to see him watching her closely. She knew he was aware.

Clark refused a second cup of coffee and said they really must be getting home.

Cam, still bragging about his boy, pushed back from the table and went with Clark for his team.

Marty smiled bravely as she bid Wanda farewell, and prayed that Clark would please hurry.

In short order the team was at the door, and Clark jumped down to help Marty into the wagon. They traveled home at a much brisker pace than they had made the journey to the Marshalls'.

"Are ya gonna make it?" Clark asked at one point, and Marty nodded, holding her hands tightly in front of her as another spasm swept over her. "I sent Cam for the doc."

Marty felt thankfulness flow through her. Her previous impatience with her husband's concern for her welfare now seemed petty and shortsighted.

The tiny baby girl arrived safely, in Doc's presence and in her mother's bed, at precisely five-twenty that afternoon.

Missie, Clare, and Arnie were all impressed with the little bundle. Clae and Nandry, too, gave an enthusiastic welcome to the new addition to the Davis family.

"Can we call her Elvira, Ma?" Missie asked.

"Iffen ya like," said Marty.

"Good. I read a story about an Elvira in a book of Mr. Whittle's. I think it's a nice name."

This was the first time Ma was not present at the birthing of one of Marty's babies. But in the days immediately following, Nandry took over the running of the household. Marty couldn't believe the young girl's efficiency.

"Nandry," she said as she rocked the baby after a feeding, "I jest don't know how we ever managed without ya."

Nandry gave a brief small smile and went back to her supper preparations.

EIGHTEEN

The New Preacher

Teacher Whittle took his new responsibility very seriously. He had drawn up careful descriptions of each likely pastoral candidate, including background, disposition, and education, and presented it to Clark and Ben.

From the eight names under consideration, the committee chose three they felt might be possibilities. Mr. Whittle, as the contact man, was commissioned to write the necessary letters. He did so with great flourish, describing in detail the community, the great pioneer fervor of its settlers, and their depth of religious conviction. The letters were sent off in due course, and the committee awaited the answers with a great deal of expectancy and some trepidation.

A letter finally arrived. The candidate appreciated their interest in him, and the position sounded indeed worthy, but after much prayer, he "did not feel the Lord leading" in their direction. Ben wondered if this meant the promised salary was not enough.

Then they heard from Candidate Number Two. He, too, found it difficult to resist such a splendid opportunity, but he was getting married in a month's time, and as his wife-to-be was a very delicate little thing, he felt he could not ask her to move so far away.

"Kinda likes his soft chair and slippers," mused Ben.

Candidate Three was finally heard from. He had considered the proposal with great care, had taken much time to think about it, and perhaps in the future he would be able to consider it, but for the present he was unable to give them an answer.

"So he's hopin' fer somethin' bigger," murmured Ben and struck the name from the list.

The other five were reconsidered. To Clark and Ben they didn't seem like the kind of men who would fit their needs, but the schoolteacher was sure of their capabilities.

"Take the Reverend Knutson here," he said with enthusiasm. "He has just graduated from seven years of study for the ministry. He would be a splendid minister."

Clark and Ben couldn't help but wonder what had taken him so long, but they finally consented to allow Mr. Whittle to contact Reverend Knutson, as well as a Reverend Thomas, whose name was also on the original list.

After some time, the Reverend Knutson wrote back to declare he was most eager to take the gospel to the people of the sin-darkened western territory.

With the prospect of a minister willing to come, a meeting of the community was called to make final plans and preparations.

The group decided to approve the selection and agreed that the pastor, too, would board at the Watleys'. Their boarder's room was a large one and could accommodate another single bed and an extra desk. Mr. Whittle was delighted with this arrangement. He could renew acquaintance with the good reverend, and it would be such a boost to his own morale to have stimulating conversation with someone of his own educational status. Really, there was a great lack of intellectuals in this community. Then, too, his calling on Tessie had been received with favor, and he was most anxious to have someone with whom he could discuss this new and exciting part of his life.

The Sunday meetings would be held in the schoolhouse. It would be cramped, but they could squeeze in, so long as there was no need to move about.

Everyone was full of excitement at the prospect of their very own minister. It would be so wonderful, so comforting, to have someone there permanently. In times of birth, death, or marriage, that's when a minister was needed—not just once or twice a year as he made his itinerate pass through the area.

Secretly, the teacher hoped it would not be too long before he personally would be standing before Pastor Knutson with his bride, Tessie, at his side.

True, he had a few things to work out yet—like where to live with a wife. He could hardly move her in with him at the Watleys', though the idea had occurred to him before it was planned that the minister would lodge there. However, he was confident these things would work themselves out.

Arrangements were made to bring the new parson out, and the people eagerly looked forward to the first church meeting. March fifteenth was the date set, and the winter months seemed to pass more quickly in anticipation of this important event in the life of the community.

———

Shortly after Baby Ellie had arrived, Ma Graham came to call. Marty was awfully glad to see her, not just to show off the new baby girl, but also to have a chance for a nice long visit. Chats with Ma were always full of news. Her face now was flushed with it.

"I declare, Marty," she beamed as they settled to cups of coffee, "I'm gonna have me another son-in-law."

Marty looked up in surprise.

"Really?" She caught some of the excitement from Ma. "Nellie?"

"Yeah, Nellie."

"I didn't know—"

"Not many did. Don't know much about it myself. Nellie doesn't say much, an' the young man—well, I'm still marvelin' thet he finally got it said, him being as tight-lipped as he is."

"Who—?"

"Shem Vickers."

"No! Really?" Marty laughed with Ma as she nodded in confirmation.

"Can ya 'magine thet!" Ma was still marveling about it all. "Never even really got to know the boy 'til the last few weeks. He's right nice—even if he don't have much to say."

Marty chuckled. "Don't s'pose the poor fellow ever had much of a chance to develop his talkin'. He sure oughta have first-rate ears, though—iffen they're not already worn out."

Ma smiled her understanding. "Yeah, Mrs. Vickers can talk 'nough fer a crowd."

"When's the weddin' to be?"

"Most as soon as thet new parson gits here. Prob'ly April."

Marty smiled and nodded. "Well, thet's really nice. I'm so happy fer 'em both."

Ma agreed. "Nellie been a right fine girl. I'm gonna miss her, but she's all excited like with the plans fer a place of her own."

"She'll make Shem a fine little wife, I'm sure of thet."

Marty passed Ma the cookies and then asked carefully, "Ma, have Ben and you talked over 'bout Tommie yet?"

Ma nodded, the smile fading some from her face. "Yeah, we talked 'bout it. Then we talked to Tom, too. Ben, he don't seem too upset 'bout it. Oh, he was at first, but then he sorta jest seemed to think—what'll be, will be. But I sure don't want Tommie hurt—nor the girl, either, fer thet matter. Oh, I wisht it were all jest a dream an' I'd wake up and it'd all be over."

Ma sat shaking her head, her eyes downcast.

"I'm sure thet it will work out," said Marty, trying to sound confident. "Tommie's a smart boy. Iffen it's not gonna work, he'll know it."

"Tommie is too far gone to see anything," Ma replied. "Never saw a young man so dew struck. Tommie wants to bring her to the house to meet Ben and me."

"Why shouldn't he?" Marty blurted out, then wondered if Ma would take offense.

"I don't know, Marty," Ma answered slowly. "Seems iffen we say he can, we sorta be puttin' our blessin' on . . . on the other, too. An' the other young'uns—sure thing they wouldn't be able to keep it quiet like, either—babble it 'round the school an' all. The whole area would know 'bout it. It's jest not a good idea—not good at all."

Marty ached for Ma in her uncertainties, but she also felt deep concern for Tommie. There just didn't seem to be any way through the situation without someone getting hurt—and maybe more than one.

"Ma, I think I'd like to have a chat with Tom again," Marty finally said. "Could ya send him on over when he's got a minute?"

"Sure—guess chattin' won't hurt nothin'—might even help some."

"Tell ya what," said Marty. "I'll send along a note with ya. Fer Tom. Thet be okay?"

Ma looked surprised but quickly agreed.

"It'll jest take a minute," said Marty, pouring Ma another cup of coffee as she spoke. "Ya jest enjoy yer coffee an' I'll be right back."

She went to the bedroom and found a sheet of paper and a pencil.

"Dear Tom," she wrote. "I think it would be good if you

could bring Owahteeka to see me. Come next Wednesday, if you can. Your friend, Marty."

Carefully she folded the sheet and returned to the kitchen. Ma tucked the note into a pocket and made no comment. Marty knew the short letter would be handed over to Tom.

School and Visits

The afternoon sun seemed weak as it shone listlessly on the winter snow. A biting wind had arisen, and Marty fretted over Missie and Clae tramping home from school in the cold.

She kept glancing nervously out the window for the two figures to appear, worried with a mother's heart that the cold might somehow detain them or return them home with frostbite.

When the two girls finally came into view, they looked cheerful and nonchalant, chattering together and not seeming to be in much of a hurry to get in out of the weather.

Marty met them at the door. "Aren't ya near froze?" she asked.

Missie looked at her with surprise, glanced around, then nodded with, "Sure is cold out."

"I know. I was worried."

" 'Bout what?"

" 'Bout you—an' Clae—comin' home in the wind."

"We're all right, Mama."

She shrugged out of her coat and had to be reminded to hang it on its peg.

"Here," Marty said, "I've heated some milk. Best warm yerselves up a bit."

141

The girls accepted the warm milk and the slice of cake that went with it.

"It was cold in school today, too," offered Clae.

"Yeah," teased Missie, "Nathan gave Clae his sweater to keep warm."

Clae flushed. "Oh yeah—well, Willie loves you."

"Does not," Missie responded heatedly. "I hate thet Willie LaHaye."

"Well, he don't hate you."

"Does too. We hate each other—him and me," Missie declared with some finality but sounding rather too comfortable with "him and me" in spite of her words.

"I don't think we should talk about *hating* each other," Marty murmured. Neither girl responded, and she decided another time was better for pursuing that lesson.

Next it appeared that Clae was changing the subject, but to Marty's dismay it turned out to be the same old one.

"Know what?" Clae announced. "Today we had honor time fer the two—boy an' girl—who got the best marks in sums and in spellin'. An' guess who got honored—had to go up front an' stand?" Marty noticed that Missie was shooting daggers at Clae with her eyes, but Clae ignored her and went on, "Had to stand right up there while everybody clapped. Guess who? Missie and Willie."

She gleefully clapped her hands together in demonstration and repeated, "Missie and Willie."

"I'm proud, Missie, thet ya got top marks," Marty interrupted, hoping to divert the conversation.

"Missie and Willie," Clae said again. "Bet ya get married when ya grow up."

"We will not." Missie bounded off her chair, spilling the remainder of her milk. "I'm gonna marry Tommie, Clae Larson, an' don't ya fergit it." She was in tears now, and as a final vent to her anger she reached for a handful of Clae's hair and yanked hard before she ran off to her room.

Now of course Clae was angry, but Marty's intervention was too late to stop the girl's initial indignant outburst. She tried to calm Clae, at the same time admonishing her not to tease Missie so much, reminding Clae that as the elder it was her responsibility to keep quarrels from starting but assuring her that Missie was wrong to pull her hair. Marty wiped up the spilled milk and went to talk to her daughter.

Missie was hard to convince that the hair pulling was not in order—a just dessert for Clae's teasing. Marty firmly informed her that it was not to happen again. The most difficult part of the talk came when Marty explained, as gently as she knew how, that Tommie was a man full grown and he might have other ideas as to whom he wished to marry. This was hard for Missie to comprehend. Tommie had always been her "best friend," she said, her voice trembling.

"I know," said Marty, "but best friends don't always grow up and git married. 'Specially when one is a grown man already and the other a little girl."

"Then I'll never, ever marry anyone," Missie vowed, "not iffen I can't marry Tommie."

Marty smoothed her hair and said she supposed that would be fine—but if Missie ever changed her mind, that was all right, too.

Missie finally wiped away the last of her tears and at her mother's bidding went to offer her apology to Clae. Within minutes the two were chattering away again as if nothing had happened.

———

When Wednesday arrived Tom appeared at Marty's door. At her invitation to come in, Tom asked, "Would ya mind comin' out," he asked, "back to the spring? We'd rather see ya private like."

Clark was away, Ellie sound asleep, and Nandry had Clare and Arnie occupied, so Marty bundled up against the cold and followed Tom outside. The air was crisp but still, so the cold was not penetrating.

Marty and Tom moved along the path to the spring without speaking. Marty wondered just what to expect. What would the girl at the other end of the trail be like?

As she approached the appointed spot, a slender figure clad in beaded buckskins turned to meet her, a long, shining black braid over one shoulder.

She's beautiful, was Marty's first thought as she looked from the dark eyes to the sensitive face. The girl's lips were slightly parted, and she stood there silently, no doubt taking Marty's measure even as Marty tried in a moment's time to measure her.

"Owahteeka," said Marty softly. It was not difficult to smile and reach out a hand. "I'm right glad to meet ya."

"And I," the Indian lass spoke carefully, "I am happy to meet you . . . Marty. Tom has told me much about you."

Marty's eyes widened in surprise.

"Ya speak English—very well."

"I went to a mission school when my mother still lived," she explained, showing little emotion about the matter.

"An' yer father—?"

"Is gone. I now live only with my grandfather. He did not wish me to continue in the mission school."

"I see."

Tom had moved over beside Owahteeka. His face shone with love and with some relief.

"Has Tommie met yer grandfather?"

"Oh no," she said quickly. "He must not."

"I'd like to," Tom interjected. "I'd like to talk to the old man, tell 'im—"

"He does not speak nor understand the white man's tongue," Owahteeka broke in.

"Well, then," said Tom, "at least I could shake his hand—could smile. And you could interpret—"

"No." Owahteeka shook her head firmly. "You must not. My grandfather—he would not wish to meet you."

"But Marty has met you. She's white an'—"

Owahteeka's dark eyes flashed. "The white lady did not lose her sons and grandsons to Indian arrows as my grandfather lost his to the white man's bullets."

Marty stepped forward and placed her hand on the young girl's arm. "We understand," she said softly. "I'm sure Tom will not try to see yer grandfather—not now, anyway. But can . . . can you *always* hide your love?" She waved a hand to include the two young people. "Can ya hide it from yer grandfather?"

"My grandfather is very old," said Owahteeka softly. "He is very old and weak. He will soon go to his fathers—he will not notice. There is no need to tell him."

"I see." As silence followed, Marty fumbled for the right words and finally just blurted it out. "An' you, Owahteeka, do you wish to . . . to marry Tommie?"

"Oh yes." The dark eyes softened as Owahteeka looked at the young man beside her. Tommie's arm encircled her waist. Who could deny the love that passed between them?

Marty swallowed a lump in her throat and turned to walk away a few paces. She came back slowly again. Her heart ached for the young people before her—of different culture, of different heritage, of different religions, of different skin color. Why had this happened? Why did they make it so difficult for themselves? What could she say or do?

She finally found her voice. "Owahteeka, I think I

understand why you and Tommie love each other. You're a lovely, sensitive girl, an' ya probably know what I think about Tommie." She looked away a moment. "I . . . I wish I could feel thet . . . thet life will treat ya both kindly iffen ya marry. I don't know. I really don't know."

Marty looked again into the perceptive eyes of the girl before her. "But this I want ya to always know. Ya can count on me fer a friend."

"Thank you," whispered Owahteeka. Marty stepped forward and embraced the girl, looked deep into Tommie's eyes, and turned back toward the path to the house.

Tears fell down her cheeks as she walked. Her mind and heart swirled with contrasting emotions. She cared deeply about Tommy and now Owahteeka.

But if it hadn't been for Ma Graham with her staunch faith and her wealth of life experience from which to draw, would she herself have made it? Was it her responsibility now to offer consolation and counsel to the older woman? She didn't know if it was her place to interfere. But before she reached the house, she had decided. She wouldn't try to persuade Ma that this marriage was the right thing, but she would try to make Ma see that Tommie's mind was not going to be changed either by trying to talk him out of it or by resisting it.

TWENTY

Bits 'n Pieces

When Clark went to town the following Saturday, he returned with the sobering news that Mrs. McDonald was gravely ill. The doc, who had been faithfully attending her, reported her problem as a severe stroke. One side was paralyzed, her speech was gone, and she was confined to her bed in serious condition. Hope for her recovery was slim.

Mrs. Nettles and Widow Gray, from town, took turns with Mr. McDonald in round-the-clock nursing. The store was put up for sale.

Marty felt sick at heart upon hearing the news. She had never particularly liked Mrs. McDonald, and the news of her illness filled her with feelings of guilt and self-reproach.

Maybe iffen I'd really tried, she told herself, *maybe I could have found a lovable woman behind the pryin' eyes and probin' tongue.*

But there was little inward relief to her in the "maybes."

"God," she prayed when she had a quiet moment, "please forgive me. I've been wrong. Help me in the future to see good in all people. To mine it out iffen it seems buried deep. An' help me to love even ones where I can't discover some good."

She sent a roast and a pie along with her condolences to Mr. McDonald. That was about all she could do, though it certainly wouldn't make amends for the past.

———

Nellie's wedding plans were progressing favorably. Shem Vickers had found his tongue and was talking more than probably he had done in all his previous years. He seemed to take great pleasure in spreading the word that he was soon to be a groom.

Mr. Wilbur Whittle was also making progress with his courtship, but he had given up his hope of being the first one to escort his bride to the altar when the new preacher arrived. He still hadn't solved the problem of where to live, therefore had withheld asking the fateful question. Tessie, not understanding what was holding him back, was becoming rather impatient.

Mr. Whittle finally dared to approach the committee that served as the school board, requesting that a residence be built at the school site. He supplied them with a list of the reasons why such a move would be advantageous.

He would be there to watch the fire in the winter.

He would be available should a student require his services apart from school hours.

It would mean less time spent on the road, and he was able to list several other worthy grounds for his request.

None of the reasons he gave was the real one, but the board, after some consideration, decided that a resident teacher would not be a bad idea and voted to take out logs over the next winter to construct a modest but adequate teacherage come the spring.

It was a step in the right direction, but it seemed rather far in the future. Mr. Whittle had hoped for action a bit sooner. He deemed it wise, for the time, to hold his tongue as far as his intention toward Miss Tessie LaHaye.

And so the matter lay. Tessie didn't exactly give up—but she did do a considerable amount of complaining to her poor mother.

———

Marty bundled Ellie against the spring wind and set off for the Grahams'. She felt the time had come to have her discussion with Ma.

With Missie and Clae off to school, Nandry would be keeping Clare and Arnie at home. *She should get out more,* Marty worried to herself. *She's getting to be a real loner.* But the company of the two small children seemed to be enough for the withdrawn young woman.

With a large family usually swarming through the Graham house, it seemed awfully quiet today. The youngsters were off to school and Tom was out working around the farm buildings, so only Nellie was left to keep Ma company during the day. Ma quickly laid aside the towels she was hand-stitching and came to take wee Ellie from Marty and unwrap her, exclaiming over her "darlin' little face, that soft-as-cream skin."

Ma looked up from Ellie to ask, "Did ya know thet Sally Anne be expectin' another—not till fall. This time Jason is hopin' fer a boy, though he sure wouldn't trade thet Elizabeth Anne fer an army of boys."

Marty smiled at the good news of an addition to the family. "How's Sally Anne keepin'?" she asked.

"Fine. She's busy as can be carin' fer Jason and thet girl of theirs."

Nellie had taken little Ellie as soon as her mother would give her up. After a bit she laid the baby in a cradle kept for little visitors—one small granddaughter in particular—and went to put on the coffee.

Marty oohed and aahed over all the household items Nellie already had prepared for her new home. Ma was piecing another quilt. Marty asked Ma who was anticipating the coming wedding the most—Nellie or her mother. They both laughed; enough of an answer, Marty felt.

The coffee was ready, and each of the three took up her sewing and prepared to visit.

They shared news from the neighborhood, expressed their concern for the McDonalds, and discussed in detail Nellie's coming wedding.

When there was a pause in the conversation, Marty brought up the subject she had really come to discuss. "Tommie came last week—like I asked him to."

Ma nodded. "Yeah, he said he'd seen ya."

"Did he also say he'd brought a friend?"

"No, he did not." Ma had stopped her sewing and was watching Marty.

"He brought . . . he brought Owahteeka with him."

Ma went even more still, and Nellie's needle also stopped.

"I asked 'im to," Marty hurried on. "I felt thet somebody should meet her an' get to know jest what kind of a girl she is. I knew it was awkward like fer her to come here, but it wouldn't be a problem jest comin' to my place."

Ma's eyes were asking Marty to quickly continue—to tell her what the girl who had captured Tom's heart was like.

Nellie said the words. "What's she like?"

"She's beautiful—lovely in every way. It's no wonder Tom has fallen so hard. She's tiny and straight as a willow. She's slim and brown, with big black eyes an' long black braids. She's educated, too—speaks English real good. She's polite . . . an' . . ."

"Oh, dear God!" whispered Ma, laying aside her sewing and bowing her head. "What are we gonna do?"

Marty stopped at the interruption and the three sat in silence.

Finally Marty said softly, "But she's sorrowin', too. She loves Tommie—I'm sure of thet. But I think . . . I think maybe Tom's the only white man she could love or trust. Her grandfather—he . . . he hates the whites and with good cause, maybe. He took Owahteeka out of the mission school after her parents were gone. Fer Tommie's sake, I think she tried to accept me, but the doubtin' was still in her eyes."

Marty waited, then said, "Still, she did try . . . fer Tommie. An' maybe . . . in time. . . . I jest don't know."

Ma had not lifted her head. She passed a careworn hand over her face. "Iffen I only knew what to do. Iffen I only knew," she murmured.

Nellie quickly said, "Don't seem no problem to me. Iffen they love each other, why shouldn't they marry?"

Ma looked up. "Indeed, young Nell," she said pointedly, "all yer seein' right now is love. Me—I see beyond—to heart-ache an' even shunnin' an' a family neither white nor brown."

Ellie fussed from the cradle, and Marty rose to get her. Had she said the right things? she wondered. Should she argue further for the young couple? No, she didn't have the right, nor the wisdom, to know if it was proper. She had told them how she saw the Indian girl—Owahteeka's strength, her love, her doubts. Now Ma—and her Lord—would have to take it from there.

Lord, you know I've been talkin' to you 'bout this nearly every day, she prayed silently as she lifted Ellie from the cradle. *Please make your way clear to everyone—to Tom and Owahteeka, to Ma and Ben, to their families. An' yes, Lord, bless her old grandfather. Help him find you 'fore he dies. . . .*

TWENTY-ONE

Reverend Knutson

Ben took a team and wagon to the train stop in the neighboring town to pick up the new preacher and bring him back. Reverend Knutson would spend two days at the small hotel getting rested after his long trip, and then he would arrive at the Watleys', where he would make his home. Belle Watley was all in a dither. Imagine! Not only did she have the distinguished honor of housing the schoolteacher but now the new preacher, as well. Belle, however, did not believe in allowing her excitement to mean overexerting herself. Though her chatter and color were at their peak, she was still content to let her daughters do the bustling about in preparation for the pastor's arrival.

Word quickly spread through the town and countryside that they had indeed gotten "their man." The reverend was resting as planned in the hotel and would be picked up by the Watleys for residence at their farmstead the following Friday. This would give him a day to settle in and prepare himself for the Lord's Day and the first meeting with his new congregation.

The whole neighborhood felt the excitement, and early on Sunday morning the teams and wagons began to stream into the school yard. Even the less faithful members of the flock turned out, except for Zeke LaHaye, though he allowed his wife and family a few hours off so they, too, could meet the preacher. There would not be sitting room for everyone, that was for sure. Fortunately the weather allowed for setting up some makeshift benches outside.

Marty was mentally prepared to see another rather small man like the teacher, thinking perhaps that was the way "they made 'em out east." The sight of the still-young Reverend Knutson provided quite a shock to all. He was tall, but that was not his outstanding feature. It was his size! And it was not the weight itself the reverend carried that was remarkable but how—or where—he carried it. He was hard put trying to cover his girth with his suit coat. His face was round and full, like a small replica of what was behind his straining coat buttons.

Seeing a round face raised the expectation that it should appear jolly—but not so the Reverend Knutson. There were no laugh lines there, no crinkles at the corners of the eyes.

Maybe he's still weary, Marty told herself. *By next Sunday he'll likely be more himself.*

The good reverend possessed a booming voice, both in word and song, and in spite of some of the hymns he chose being unfamiliar to the rest of them, the singing went well. His prayer, too, was very meaningful to Marty. It sounded as though he was on good speaking terms with the Almighty. Marty felt her soul moved and her spirit warmed as the congregation worshiped together under the leadership of Reverend Knutson.

The sermon left Marty somewhat puzzled, though. The reverend had a voice that was easy enough to listen to, but some of the words and ideas were unfamiliar and difficult for Marty to grasp. Just when she felt perhaps she knew what he was saying, she would get lost again. She chided herself for her ignorance and determined to check with Clark on the way home.

There was general visiting and introductions as the people filed out of the schoolhouse. Marty heard several comments of

"Good sermon, Parson," and was more convinced than ever that she was terribly dull.

On the way home she put it to Clark. "Reverend Knutson's jest fine, ain't he?"

"Seems so."

"Got a nice voice that carries even to the outside, hasn't he?"

" 'Deed he has."

"Sings real good, too."

"Fine singer."

"Clark—what *was* he talkin' 'bout?"

Clark started to laugh.

"Be hanged iffen I know," he finally managed through his mirth.

"Ya don't know, either?"

"Haven't a notion," said Clark. "Don't s'pose there be a soul there who did."

"Thought it was jest me thet's dumb," admitted Marty, and Clark laughed again.

"Well," he said, getting himself under control, "I think the good parson was sayin' somethin' about man bein' a special creature, designed fer a special purpose, but I never did get rightly sorted out what thet purpose was. 'Fulfillment of man's higher purpose' or some such thing seems to have come up more than once. Not sure what he's meanin'."

Marty sat quietly.

"Maybe next Sunday he'll explain," she said thoughtfully. She decided right then and there that she'd be praying for Reverend Knutson as he fit himself into the community and their needs. She truly wanted their children—all the children, actually—to receive further spiritual nurture and training now that they had a regular pastor.

Marty was clearing away the supper dishes when she heard a lone horse approaching. Tommie swung down from the saddle, appearing to be in a great hurry. Marty prayed that nothing was wrong as she rushed to the door to meet him.

His face was white and drawn and there was a determined set to his chin.

"Can I see ya?" he asked, his tone as tense as his expression.

"Of course, Tommie," she said, drawing him inside, then asking quickly, "Tommie, what's wrong?"

"I'm leavin'."

"Leaving! Fer where? Why?"

"I'm goin' west."

"But why?"

"I got a note this afternoon from Owahteeka. We were to meet as usual, but she wasn't there. I waited an' waited an' I got worried, an' then jest as I was gonna go find her—grandfather or no—I spotted these stones piled up—an' in 'em a letter."

He shoved the crumpled paper toward Marty, and she took it with trembling fingers.

Dear Tommie,
    Grandfather must have learned of us. He is taking me back to the reservation. Please don't try to follow. It would mean danger. I am promised to Running Deer as his wife.
                            Owahteeka.

"Oh, Tommie!" Marty whispered. "I'm so sorry." She now understood the anguish in the young man's face.

Tom shuffled around, and Marty realized he was fighting for control of his emotions.

"But why . . . why go away?" she finally asked him.

"I won't stay here." There was bitterness in his voice. "This is jest what Ma wanted. She should be happy now."

Marty laid a hand on his arm, feeling the muscles tense with his anger and grief.

"Tommie, no mother is ever happy when their young'uns are in pain. Can't ya see thet? Oh, I know Ma was worried, worried 'bout you an' Owahteeka. She didn't feel it was right. But yer hurtin', Tommie—an' yer sorrow will never make her happy. She's gonna be in terrible pain, too, Tommie—truly she is."

Tommie wiped the back of his hand across his face and half turned from Marty.

"I still gotta go," he said eventually, his voice hoarse. "I jest can't stay here—thet's all. Every day I'll think I see Ma lookin' through me, sortin' me out, wishin' me to find another girl. . . ."

"I see," Marty answered gently.

"I left 'em a note. Didn't say much. You tell 'em, will ya, Marty? Try to tell 'em why I had to go."

Marty couldn't speak over the lump in her throat but agreed with a nod of her head. "Be careful, Tommie, ya hear," she whispered, "an' write a note now and then, will ya?"

He nodded but said nothing further. He turned and was gone. Marty was left standing in the doorway, watching him go, while tears streamed down her cheeks.

TWENTY-TWO

Life Moves On

Tom's departure was very hard on the young Missie. His family and friends were left with deep inward sorrow because of it, but along with the pain in Missie's heart was deep confusion. It was simply beyond her comprehension that Tommie would choose to leave everyone—to leave her. Marty tried to explain, but her efforts were in vain.

Ma's aching heart was hidden by the attention and activities required for Nellie's wedding. Marty watched her bustling about, organizing everything that needed to be done, but she knew beneath Ma's smile and her instructions to everyone within sight and sound was a mother's heart broken for her grief-stricken son.

When March was torn from the general store calendar and discarded, April promised new growth, new life, new vigor. Nellie plunged into the last-minute preparations with flushed cheeks and a beaming face.

"Do folks always smile when they gonna marry?" Clare wondered after a Sunday morning service in which he had spent more time watching those around him than listening to the reverend.

Marty chuckled. "Mostly," she said, "mostly they do."

Clare shrugged and let it go at that. The "why" of the whole matter quite escaped him.

Reverend Knutson had by now presented five sermons to his congregation, and Marty had long since given up on any reasonable explanation of his meaning. Others seemed to have given up, also, and a few of the less ardent families had ceased to attend. The schoolroom was still overcrowded, however, and the worship service wasn't always as worshipful as many wished it to be.

Marty did wish the reverend weren't quite so educated, so formal. She longed so much for spiritual nourishment, similar to what she found during the daily Bible reading with Clark and their family. Sunday by Sunday she went home feeling uncertain and agitated. She was sure she was hearing truth in those fancy phrases, but she did wish that truth could be presented in a way she could take home with her and apply to her life.

The Davis family had invited Reverend Knutson to join them for a Sunday dinner. Never had she seen a man tuck away as much fried chicken or mashed turnips. She of course said nothing and continued to pass the serving bowls his way, but when she saw Clare watching him in wide-eyed disbelief, she suppressed a giggle and quickly diverted Clare's attention lest he blurt out some embarrassing remark.

Marty and Clark talked about the situation over those early weeks. They decided to accept their new minister—accept him for who he was, for whom he represented, for what he had come to do. He had come a very long way to teach them from the Bible, and certainly they could open their hearts to the Word of God and trust Him for the rest.

———

When school began again that fall, along with the girls trudged small Clare, self-confident and assured. His only concern was how Clark would manage the farm without him. But when Clark told him he supposed he could make do—he had Arnie now—Clare nodded reluctant agreement.

He was full of tales of school, often about some lark or humorous playground happening or classroom mishap. Missie occasionally accused him of being a downright tattletale, but that did not dampen Clare's enthusiasm for a good story.

One day Marty sat in the quietness of the house knitting a new pair of mittens before winter set in. Nandry was off picking blueberries in the far pasture, Arnie was "helping" his dad, the three school children were at school, and Baby Ellie was having her nap.

Marty's thoughts turned to Wanda. By now the whole community was aware that little Rett was not progressing normally—everyone, it seemed, but Wanda and Cam. Marty's heart felt heavy as she thought of the boy. Though finally walking on his own, he still did not attempt to speak, and it was evident he would never be like other children.

Cam still boasted about his son. "See how big and strong he is?" he would ask anyone within earshot. How would he take it, Marty wondered, when he finally realized the truth?

Marty was surprised to look up from her thoughts to see Wanda herself driving into the yard. She had brought Rett with her, and he sat upright beside her on the wagon seat, delightedly holding the end of the reins beyond where she grasped them.

Wanda tied the team and lifted the big boy down. He shuffled about the yard and became excited at the sight of Ole Bob. The boy and the dog soon became acquainted.

Then Wanda took the boy's hand and led him toward the house. He did not protest, but he did not show any eagerness, either.

Wanda wasted no time with small talk. "I had to see you, Marty," she began. Marty noticed her quivering chin.

"I know the neighbors are all talking about Rett being different," she said, her voice shaking. "I know they are. I know, too, that they think . . . they think Cam and I aren't aware. We know, Marty, we know. I guess I've known from the time Rett was a tiny baby. Oh, I hoped and prayed that I'd be wrong . . . but I knew. For a while I wondered . . . I wondered about Cam. I wondered when he'd learn the truth . . . how he'd feel when he did. And then . . . one night . . . well, he just spilled it all out. He'd known, too."

Wanda stopped and her hand went to her lips. She took a deep breath, then went on, "Marty, have you . . . have you ever seen a grown man cry? I mean really cry? It's awful . . . just awful."

Wanda wiped away her tears, took a breath, and continued, her voice stronger now. "I felt I just had to share with someone . . . someone who would understand. It was hard at first . . . really hard. But, Marty, I want you to know I wouldn't change it, not really. He has brought us so much joy. You see"—she looked at Marty, the tears glistening in her eyes—"I asked God so many times for a baby. And . . . and He's given me one—a boy that will, in some respects, never grow up. Now, can I fault God for answering my prayer? I don't suppose, Marty, that Rett will ever leave me, not even for school. I have . . . I have my baby . . . for always."

"Oh, Wanda." Marty went to put her arms around her friend, and they wept together. When their tears had washed through the grief, they were able to talk of other things.

Rett played contentedly with the building blocks, pushing them back and forth on the kitchen floor, for he couldn't seem to succeed in stacking them.

TWENTY-THREE

Church and Family

The small log teacherage was built the following spring, and Mr. Wilbur Whittle and his bride moved into their new little home. The community had long since realized the true reason for Mr. Whittle's insistence on a home of his own near the schoolhouse, for immediately after receiving assurances it would indeed be built, he asked for the hand of Miss Tessie. The community smiled its approval, and as the finishing touches were put on the teacherage, Reverend Knutson did the honors of pronouncing the couple husband and wife.

Among the members of the community, though, was a growing dissatisfaction with the Sunday morning worship service. Rather than laying the fault on the "learned man" and his lofty sermons, the people instead felt the problem was related to the place of meeting. The school was crowded, the seating was inadequate, and there was no place to take fussing children. That the situation was not conducive to worship was the thrust of neighborhood discussions.

In between the planting of crops and the haying season, a meeting was organized to discuss the matter. The turnout was strong, and many expressed their feeling that the community was in dire need of a proper church. Then followed a lengthy discussion as to where this building should be located. Several generously offered land, but the group finally decided the most central location would be a corner of the Watley farm. Come fall, a group of volunteers would pace off and fence the area. Another group would take up the task of log count. Then throughout the winter months, men and horses would strain and sweat getting the lumber transformed from tall standing timber in the hills to stripped logs in ever-increasing piles at the building site. Clark would oversee the job of sorting the logs to make sure the number snaked in would be adequate for the building.

Wooden benches would satisfy the seating of those full-grown men who had, Sunday by Sunday, been forced to squeeze their tall frames into desks created for fifth graders. An altar would provide a place where those with spiritual needs could bow in prayer, and the Word of God would be proclaimed from a specially fashioned pulpit.

All of the plans drew great excitement from the group, and all went home from the meeting with spirits lifted. Now they were finally getting somewhere. Their worship time surely would have a better chance of meeting their needs with an appropriate gathering place. The church would be much larger than the schoolhouse. It would have two side rooms, one where the children could be taught in a Sunday school class and a smaller one where crying babies would not disturb the rest of the congregation.

The reverend seemed to agree with the plans, though he did not show any particular enthusiasm. He was quick to inform the group of the great number of hours needed in his study for the purpose of preparing himself for his Sunday sermon. The clear message was that it was fine with him as long as he was not called upon for some such task as log cutting.

So be it, the planners concluded. After the crops had been harvested and the fall work completed, the menfolk took to the wooded hills. Their family's wood supply had to be secured first, and they were in a hurry to complete the task so they could start tallying up the logs for the new church.

As the winter wore on, each day that was fit for man and beast to be out carried the sharp sound of axes and the crashing of large timbers. Gradually the piles of logs at the site grew, and Clark, who was keeping the tally and overseeing the peeling, reported to Marty the steady progress they were making.

With the spring thaw, large piles of naked, steaming logs lay in the warm spring sun. A day in May was set aside for the church raising. Because it was special and larger than most of the buildings they had erected, the men knew the church would take more than one day to see completion, but the first day would give them a sense of direction, the raw outline with which to work.

The community met on the appointed day, and the men set to work, grouping rather naturally into teams for the various endeavors required to put up their meetinghouse. The women chatted and cooked and chased hungry children out of the food set aside for dinner. By evening as the farmers headed for home to their waiting chores, the walls of the church stood stout and strong. Those who could take the time agreed to come the next day to work again on the building. The important things now were to get the roof on, the windows in, and the door hung. The finishing on the inside would be done throughout the spring and summer as men could spare the time.

By fall their church stood tall, even bearing a spire pointing one and all to heaven. "Only a bell is lacking," noted some who remembered such traditions back east.

To the east of the church a cemetery was carefully staked out. As she watched the men plotting the area, Marty wondered if any others carried the same question in their hearts: *Who would be the first to be laid to rest there?*

She tried to brush it aside, but in spite of herself her eyes traveled over her neighbors. She loved them. She did not want to lose any of them. Then she caught sight of her own family, and she found herself choking up a bit.

I'm bein' silly, she scolded herself. *Our lives are all in God's hands. He'll do the choosin'.*

She went to join Clark, who was attempting to hold a squirming Ellie as she tried to get down to run with the rest of the small fry. *Yes, Lord,* Marty prayed silently as she watched the toddler go after a ball that came her way, *we're all in your care. We'll do our best to be careful and wise, but you are the one who's watchin' over us all.*

The dedication of the new church would take place on the first Sunday in October. They all decided they'd make a real celebration of it and bring in a potluck meal.

When the great day arrived, the wind was blowing and the sky was overcast, making the day less favorable than desired, but Marty was thankful that at least there was no rain falling.

She packed with care the food she had prepared and made sure her family was warmly clothed against the weather. As usual, Arnie was hard to corner long enough to be sure he was properly buttoned with cap firmly on his head. "I ain't cold," he muttered as they went to the wagon for the trip to the church.

A larger-than-usual crowd poured into the churchyard, full of great expectation. They now had a church in which to worship.

The congregation enjoyed singing the familiar hymns. By now they also knew some of the new songs the reverend had brought with him.

The prayer was long and elaborate. Marty found herself praying her own more simple one that met the need of her own heart.

Then began the dedication service for the new building.

Clark, Ben, and Mr. Watley each had a part. Marty thought it was beautiful, and her heart swelled with pride as she watched Clark participate.

Now ya watch yer pa, her expression said to their youngsters sitting on either side. *See how straight he stands—how steady his voice—how proud he is to be a part of God's people. Watch yer pa.* They seemed to catch her meaning, and even little Ellie sat silent on her mother's lap, earnest eyes fastened on Clark's face.

Oh, dear God, make it special. Make it a time for feedin' our souls, Marty prayed when the sermon began. But the dear reverend hadn't gone far into the message before she realized she was going to again be disappointed. She settled back to hear out the sermon with at least attentiveness if not with understanding.

The reverend must have felt the sermon on such a splendid occasion also should be special, so he had prepared an extra long one.

Children were beginning to fidget, and Marty couldn't help but feel that some fathers probably felt a bit envious of the mothers who got to take them into the new crying room.

At last the sermon ended, and the congregation stood for the closing hymn. The people filed from the building—the men to gather in small clusters, the children to stretch muscles cramped from so long a time unused, and the women to put out the noonday meal.

In spite of the long service and the unfriendly weather, it turned out to be a very pleasant time spent together. As true among friends, there was frequent good-natured banter, babies were passed around and exclaimed over, news from town and community was exchanged. It was a good day.

———————

A short note had arrived from Tommie. It was the third time the Davises had heard from him. With each letter Marty breathed a prayer of thanks that he was still safe. This letter told them he was doing fine. He planned to stay where he was for the winter—working in a lumber mill. Thought he would push on farther west come spring. Maybe even to the coast. Hadn't had himself a look at the ocean yet. He sent his love.

The envelope showed no return address, and even the postage stamp was blurred, so they were none the wiser as to his whereabouts. Marty had hoped to respond in writing, letting him know they wished him well and hoped he would soon be returning home.

Marty read the letter aloud at mealtime with their family around the table. Clark had already read it previously, but she could tell he was listening carefully as she read it again. She could see his relief and his care for the young lad in his expression.

The long months since Tom had left had erased much of the sorrow from young Missie's heart. She now seemed to think little about the young man who was suddenly gone from her life—the one she had childishly pledged herself to marry.

Marty looked with interest about the table at each of them. Actually, they all had changed during the time since Tom had left. She supposed he had changed, too.

Nandry, now a young lady, was still quiet, though always industrious. Marty had eventually given up attempts to get close to the reserved girl and accepted her as she was. *Bless her heart,* thought Marty, *in her own way she's fit into our family.* A small smile touched her lips as she silently noted, *She's been worth her keep an' thet ten dollars over and over again.*

Marty was well aware that Nandry would likely be moving along into adulthood and her own home before long. At least two of the neighborhood boys were busy studying the girl, Marty had seen. And, Marty observed, Nandry's cheeks flushed and an unusual twinkle sparkled in her eye at the attention.

Clae, too, was almost a young lady. She was nearing the completion of her education in the one-room school but not anywhere near the end of her hunger for knowledge. Marty and Clark had lain in bed nights quietly discussing her future. Her burning desire was to become a teacher, and Clark felt that even though many dollars would be involved, Clae should be given the opportunity. She would have to go away to continue her education and get her teaching certificate. As much as Marty yearned for Clae's happiness, she dreaded the thought of her leaving them.

Missie was eleven now—still a bundle of energy that was one minute a little girl and the next minute stretching toward womanhood. She loved school; in fact, Missie welcomed each new venture whether at home, on the farm, or in the classroom. She still did not like Willie LaHaye, she announced occasionally.

Clare, at nine, was a bright boy who still preferred *doing* to learning, though there was nothing wrong with his ability in either area. He still mimicked Clark and watched carefully to see how his pa handled situations.

So it's been more'n nine years, Marty continued her musings, *since Clark rescued me at the side of a broken-down wagon and a fresh-dug grave.* . . . But she didn't linger long with those memories. She could feel Clark's eyes watching her, and she turned to look at him and share a smile across the table. He still insisted "if there was any rescuin' to be doin', it was Missie and me that needed it."

Marty now turned back quickly to snatch Arnie's cup of milk from the edge of disaster. At almost six, he was their outgoing and very busy little boy, and scrapes of various kinds seemed to follow him around. He was going to be allowed to attend school this fall, which Marty was anticipating with mixed emotions.

Three-year-old Ellie was a small bundle of brightness in everybody's life. Happy and playful, she darted among them like a small butterfly, enriching the lives of all she touched.

In the family cradle rested new Baby Luke. More than once Marty had sincerely thanked God for Nandry's help since the arrival of little Luke, for unlike her others, this baby was a fussy one, demanding attention just at the time when a mother was the busiest. Nandry did her best to comfort the cranky infant.

My family, thought Marty, once more looking round the table. *My strange, wonderful family.* Lest she become teary-eyed with emotion just thinking of each one, she herded her thoughts back to safer ground and went on with her meal.

"Saw Cam today," Clark said between mouthfuls of food.

"Did ya?"

"He had Rett with 'im. Do ya know thet thet boy can already handle a team? Should've seen Cam. Proud as punch. Says Rett's gonna be the best horseman in these here parts. Might just be, too. Seems to be a natural with animals."

"Isn't thet somethin'." Marty marveled at the good news.

"Cam says he wouldn't be none surprised to see thet lad take 'im on the tamin' of even a bear. Never says a word, but he seems to make the animals understand 'im.

"Mr. Cassidy at the store says Cam never comes to town but he brings Rett either on the wagon beside 'im or up in front of 'im in the saddle."

Clark seemed to be deep in thought for a moment. "Funny thing," he then said, "Cam's changed. Watchin' 'im move about town with his son, I noticed a thoughtfulness 'bout 'im. He ain't thinkin' jest on Cam Marshall no more. I think others note it, too. Seem to have new respect fer 'im someway. Thought as I watched 'im leavin' town with thet boy up there beside 'im handlin' the reins, 'There goes a real man.'"

Marty nodded, her eyes misting over a bit, but mostly her

thoughts were of Wanda and the happiness she would feel in having given Cam a son he could love and proudly bring with him to town in spite of his difficulties.

"Did ya happen to see Mr. McDonald when you were in town?" she asked. Mrs. McDonald had passed away two years previously, having never recovered from her stroke. Mr. Mc-Donald had decided after her funeral to sell the store to Mr. Cassidy and return east, but time had brought him back to the area.

"Yeah. Saw 'im sittin' on the bench out in front of the store with Ole Tom and Jake Feidler. Didn't talk to 'im much more'n a howdy."

"How'd he seem?"

"Pretty good. I think he be right glad to be back. He jest didn't feel to home there," Clark went on to explain. Mr. McDonald had taken a room at Mrs. Keller's boardinghouse and now spent his days chatting, whittling, and spitting tobacco juice out in front of his old store. Mr. Cassidy didn't seem to mind, though Mrs. Cassidy was probably tired of scrubbing the steps.

Marty fleetingly wondered what it would be like to return east after having been away so long. Her own pa was gone now, and her ma lived alone. They kept in touch, though mail delivery meant the letters they exchanged were sometimes far between. Marty did try to keep her posted on each new grandchild and to send her greetings at Christmastime.

No, she was sure she wouldn't feel at home back east anymore, either.

She gently but firmly moved Arnie's fingers away from the butter and gave him a piece of buttered bread. The years had brought so many changes—most of them good ones, she decided.

———

Young Josh Coffins was the first to show serious intentions toward Nandry. Marty knew it was bound to come, and she welcomed it and despaired over it at the same time. She knew Nandry longed for a home and family of her own, yet the Davis family would have a large hole in it without her. Marty and Ma Graham had some long chats about these kinds of changes in a family and how to set one's heart and mind on the good.

Josh approached Clark after church one Sunday to ask permission to call.

"Sure thing, Josh," Clark said, clapping the young man on the shoulder, "I'd be most happy to have ya drop by to see me. Reckon we could have us a quiet talk—maybe out in the barn where we'd not be interrupted by small fry and women." Clark did enjoy his teasing.

Josh reddened and stammered as he tried to explain that wasn't really what he had in mind. Clark laughed and once more good-naturedly slapped him on the back, and Josh realized that he'd been "had."

Josh laughed at the joke on himself, and he appeared to feel good that this respected man of the community would take time to joke around with him.

"Yer welcome to come," Clark said more seriously, "an' I promise not to be holdin' ya at the barn."

Josh grinned, muttered his thanks, and walked away. Marty lingered nearby, furtively watching his approach to Nandry. He came up to her as she sat on the church steps, several youngsters around her. Baby Luke was on her lap, pointing out horses and wagons with his usual "Wha' dat?"

Josh leaned over the handrail. Nandry looked up, and the color of her face deepened.

"Been talkin' to Clark," Marty could hear him say. It had

always been "Mr. Davis" till now, but the way had been cleared for a new relationship.

Nandry's eyes widened at his words.

"He says it's fine with 'im if I come callin'."

Nandry's color deepened still more, but she said nothing.

"Is it all right with you?" There, the question was out. The ball was now handed to Nandry. There was no way she could pretend not to understand his meaning. She flushed a deep red and studied the child on her lap. Minutes ticked by. It no doubt seemed an eternity to Josh, who stood waiting, heart pounding and hands sweating. Marty certainly hadn't intended to eavesdrop, but now she could not move away without drawing attention to herself. She held her breath. What would Nandry say?

"I reckon" finally came the soft answer, and Josh's face broke into a relieved grin.

"Thanks," he said to Nandry, sounding surprisingly calm. "Thanks. Next Wednesday, then. I'll be lookin' forward to it," and then he was gone, probably suppressing the urge to run and leap over the nearby pump.

Nandry buried her blushing face against the small Luke. Later that day she was surprisingly forthcoming with Marty, and she said she'd been hoping it would be Josh. She had noticed Willis Aitkins looking at her, too, but she really favored Josh.

"He isn't even waitin' for Saturday," she noted to Marty with wonder in her voice. Usually when young folks started to keep company, the calls were made on Saturday night. Only the very serious called on *both* Saturday and Wednesday.

Nandry was watching Marty's face very carefully, her eyes begging for Marty's approval.

Marty put her arms around the young woman, noting with a pang that they were now the same height. "Oh, Nandry," she said, "I am happy for you, and I'm sad for me."

Nandry hugged her back with genuine warmth, then turned quickly away in embarrassment to swing small Luke up in her arms and hold him so closely he squirmed in protest.

"Oh, Lukey." Marty knew Nandry called him that only when she felt especially affectionate. "How can one feel so happy, an' sad, an' excited, an' scared all at one time?"

Luke didn't understand the question, but he reached out his little hand to touch the tear that lay glistening on her cheek.

TWENTY-FOUR

Christmas

As Marty made preparations for the coming Christmas, she felt this would be a very special celebration. As much as she appreciated this time of year, never before had Marty felt such anticipation.

Baby Luke, a happy child, scurried about, having outgrown his early colicky fussiness. Ellie was still their bright butterfly, but now small bits of her boundless energy were being channeled into productive and helpful activities. Arnie, Clare, and Missie would enjoy the holiday from school and were already making plans for sliding on the creek's frozen surface and sledding down its banks. But the most important item adding to the extra excitement was that Clae would be home—Clae, their young teacher-in-the-making. Marty could hardly wait till she arrived, and she could tell that Nandry also was anticipating seeing her sister again.

Clae's letters from normal school were filled with excitement about what she was learning, who she was meeting, but most important, how much she was missing them all.

Marty fussed over all Clae's favorite dishes, made sure Nandry had their shared room prepared, and encouraged the younger children to feel the same excitement she felt. There would be a new face at their Christmas table, as well. Josh Coffins, Nandry's promised, would be joining them. Marty shared in the joy of the young couple along with dismay at the thought of losing her Nandry.

A spring wedding was planned, and as soon as the rush of Christmas was behind them, Nandry and Marty would get down to the serious business of preparing the bridal dowry.

Nandry looked very happy, and Marty had for some months been giving her the egg money so she would have something with which to buy the little extras for her first home of her own.

But first Marty would feast upon Christmas.

Clark chose the tree and some evergreen boughs that would form their traditional wreaths.

Nandry had added a half-dozen turkeys to her chicken pens, so one of them would grace the table. She selected a fine young gobbler, and it was getting extra daily care and attention.

Pies, tarts, and cookies, along with loaf cakes, lined the shelves in the pantry.

Marty had been to town for her shopping, and gifts lay wrapped beside her chest of drawers and hidden beneath her bed to supply the socks hung above the mantel for Christmas morning.

On the day Clae was to arrive, both Nandry and Marty were almost too excited to work. Eventually Marty decided she was glad she had so much to do to help the time go faster. Still it seemed the clock would never get around to four o'clock, when Clark and the team were expected back from the train station.

At last Marty heard Ole Bob's sharp bark and the happy shouts of children.

Missie burst into the house. "Guess who we found?" she teased.

They all came tramping in, Clark carrying Clae's suitcase and a large bag.

Marty pulled the girl into her arms.

"Oh, Clae, jest look at ya. Why, ya've gone and plumb growed up on us since ya been away."

Clae hugged her in return, laughing as she pointed out it had only been three months. "But oh, it's so good to be home. I could hardly wait," she added.

Clae went from Marty to her sister and then to Ellie and Luke, hugging each one in turn and exclaiming over how the youngsters had all grown. Nandry's cheeks flushed with Clae's teasing about her Josh, but she looked pleased.

"I'm thinkin'," said Clark over the joyful commotion, setting down the suitcase and the bundle, "thet we're in need of a bigger house."

Marty just smiled. They were hard put for space at times, she knew. She was once again having to put up with a crib in their bedroom, and the three girls who shared one room barely had room to turn around.

They were crowded, but they were happy. The lively conversation did not lessen as the evening wore on. There were so many things for Clae to tell, to describe. There were so many questions for the others to ask.

After the young ones had been put to bed with the promise of full Christmas socks in the morning, Marty, Nandry, and Clae still talked on, Clark nearby adding an occasional comment or question.

"When is the day for your wedding?" Clae asked Nandry, and Marty noticed Clae's careful speech.

"The last of May. We wanted to wait 'til ya'd be home. You're to be my maid o' honor, ya know."

"I hoped I would. Where are you going to live?"

"There's a small cabin on the Coffins' farm. The people who used ta own the farm lived in it. The Coffins built a bigger one when they came. We'll use the little'un fer now."

"You must be excited."

"I am," said Nandry, and her smile confirmed it. "It's a funny feelin'. I want so much fer time to go quickly, yet I don't want it to at the same time."

"Meanin'?" Clae forgot herself for the moment, using the familiar expression.

"This house—the little'uns—I really hate to leave the kids."

Marty marveled at the more frequent glimpses they had been getting of Nandry's heart.

"You won't be too far away," said Clae. She shook her head and sighed. "No one will ever know how homesick I was at first. I thought I'd just die if I didn't get home. I thought I'd never make it—but I did. I reminded myself of the money being paid for my schooling—the faith that people have in me . . . and . . . and I remembered our ma, too, Nandry. Sometimes I think about Ma, about how proud she'd be, how happy that we're getting a chance."

Yes, Marty was sure Mrs. Larson would be proud of her two daughters.

"She'd be happy for both of us," Clae went on "—for me being a teacher, for you marrying Josh. It sort of gives it extra meaning, remembering Ma."

It was the first time the girls had ever talked about their mother in Marty's presence.

"Yer ma would be very proud." Marty spoke softly. "She wanted so much thet ya both make good, an' ya have, both of ya, an' I'm proud, too."

Clae put her arms around Marty's neck and gave her an affectionate squeeze.

"And we know why," she said. "We haven't said much maybe—not as much as we should, but we know why we've made good. Thank you—thank you so much. I do love you, and I'll never forget . . . never."

Nandry nodded her head in agreement, her expression saying more than words.

————

The household was awakened early by Arnie's squeals of delight. Clare's voice soon joined his and then the general commotion followed. Marty pulled herself out of bed and slipped into her house socks and robe. Clark was already on his feet, tucking his shirt into his trousers. They entered the sitting room at the same time Nandry came in carrying Luke, barely awake. Ellie danced, 'round the room waving her arms, so caught up in Arnie and Clare's excitement at their bulging stockings she had not even thought to check out what her own might hold.

Luke quickly rubbed the sleep out of his eyes and stood transfixed, gazing at the tree in the corner that had sprung up from somewhere during the night.

Missie finally emerged, yawning and complaining about the noise.

"It's not even five o'clock," she said in disbelief. "Ya used ta make me wait a lot longer than this when I was little."

"They'd've waited, too, iffen I'd had anything to do with it," responded Clark, but Marty noticed that he seemed to be enjoying the whole pleasant uproar.

Eventually the fire was kindled in the kitchen stove and the kettle put on to boil. Clark replenished the fireplace and coaxed it to flame. Calm again reigned in the Davis household.

The older ones took advantage of the near quiet to exchange their gifts. Clae had somehow managed to bring a small gift for each of them. Marty knew she did not have much extra spending money and appreciated her gift the more for it. What Clae had lacked in dollars she had supplied with creativity, and her sewing skills had come to the fore. Luke hugged a stuffed teddy bear. Ellie wore a pint-sized apron complete with a pocket. Arnie and Clare eyed their checkered man-sized handkerchiefs, pleased that the squares matched their pa's. For Missie there was a lace-trimmed bonnet, and Nandry opened a carefully embroidered pair of pillowcases for her hope chest. Marty unwrapped the most beautiful lace handkerchief she had ever seen, but the note that accompanied the gift was what made Marty cry, for it bore the simple words *To Mother, with love, Clae.* None of her children had ever called her anything but Ma, and it seemed very meaningful for this special girl to use the more formal title.

Clark's gift handkerchief carried sentiment, too, and he slipped the card that accompanied it into Marty's hand. The card read, *Thanks for being a true pa. Love, Clae.*

Marty tried to blink away the bittersweet tears in her eyes as she thought of the one who had not been "a true pa" to his daughters. What a privilege for Clark and her to fill in as mother and father to them.

Nandry, too, had surprises for them. She had made picture books for all the younger children, gluing newspaper and calendar pictures she had gathered onto pieces of cloth. Missie received new hair ribbons, which still delighted her feminine senses. Marty got a little wooden box to hold her many and varied recipes that were forever overflowing the drawer where she kept them. Clark received a handmade cover for the well-worn family Bible.

Marty and Clark then passed out their presents for each of their family members and watched with pleasure the shining eyes of the recipients.

The clutter was cleared away, the cherished gifts put carefully in their new owners' places, and the day's celebrations proceeded.

After breakfast Clare and Arnie went out to try the new sled Clark had made them. Ellie, apron-clad to Clae's delight, was playing with her tiny set of new dishes, and Luke was put back to bed to catch up on some sleep.

Missie, feeling quite grown-up, joined the women in the kitchen, where she helped prepare the Christmas dinner.

Josh just didn't seem to be able to stay away and arrived earlier than expected. He shyly offered Nandry his gift, a new lamp to be used in their home. Marty told him she had never seen a prettier one. A soft cluster of roses was painted on the bowl in reds and pinks, and the chimney was generously trimmed with gold. Whatever it was Nandry presented to Josh the family was not allowed to see, but Marty had her suspicions that it was a mustache cup. Josh was carefully nurturing a mustache that he hoped to have full and well groomed by his wedding day, making him look more manly.

They roasted chestnuts at the fire and sniffed hungrily at the inviting fragrances coming from the kitchen. Just before the meal was set on the table, the family gathered for the reading of the Christmas story. Even Luke, from his spot on Nandry's knee, appeared to listen. Marty looked around the room at all the faces intent on Clark as he read, and her heart filled with praise to God. She slipped her hand into Clark's during his prayer, and he pressed her fingers firmly in his own.

Just as the chairs were being placed around the table, Ole Bob began to bark. It was unusual to have unexpected guests on Christmas Day, and Marty felt her heart flutter. She hoped nothing was wrong. She followed Clark to the door, almost afraid to look out.

She could hear footsteps approaching the door, and with barely a knock the door pushed open.

"Tommie," was all she could say.

"Tommie," echoed Clark, sounding equally incredulous. "Good to see ya, boy," he said, welcoming the young man with a bear hug.

Then it was Marty's turn—followed by greetings all round, excitedly and with great enthusiasm.

"Jest a minute," Tommie said, holding up his hand. "I got somethin' to show ya."

He was gone but soon back with his arm around a small young woman, her brown curls captured under a blue bonnet.

"My wife," he said with pride. "My wife, Fran."

"Oh, Tommie," exclaimed Marty. "Tommie, when did ya marry? Why didn't ya write?"

Tommie laughed. "Five months ago now. I wanted to surprise ya. Isn't she somethin'?" He looked at her again and his arm tightened. Fran smiled shyly.

"I'm pleased to meet ya all," she finally said, putting out one small hand to Clark and then Marty.

Marty stepped forward to give her a warm embrace.

"An' we are jest so glad to meet you. Won't ya come in? Take off yer coats. We are jest sittin' down, an' we are so pleased to have ya join us."

"No, no," said Tom, "we haven't been home yet. Since we were comin' right by here, I wanted ya to meet her. But we must move along. Ma might forgive me for stoppin' here on the way, but she'd never fergive me iffen I stopped here to eat Christmas dinner."

"Oh, it's gonna be so hard to let ya go now. I've so many questions—"

"They'll keep," Tommie interjected. "We'll be around. I decided I'd take up thet piece of land o' mine. See iffen I can make a farm outta it. Fran's ma and pa owned a store out west. Now there's a switch, huh?" he winked. " 'Long comes a guy, marries their daughter, an' takes her *east*."

"Oh, Tommie! I know the both of you'll be so happy."

"Thet we already are," Tommie assured her, and his eyes said it was true.

They bid their good-byes and promised to be back soon for a nice long visit.

"Well, this has truly been some day." Marty expressed the feelings of them all as the family returned to their Christmas dinner.

They bowed their heads and Clark's deep voice spoke reverently to their Father, thanking Him for the many blessings that life held, and especially for Tommie, a son come home and the joy that this would bring to the Graham household.

Marty wondered briefly about the pretty Owahteeka. Had she found happiness with her Running Deer? Marty prayed that she had.

TWENTY-FIVE

One More Time

Finally the people of the community reluctantly admitted to themselves and to one another that the highly trained Reverend Knutson simply was not fitting in, nor was he meeting the needs of the congregation.

Once they had admitted this fact, they wondered why it had taken them so long to put it on the table. What to do about the problem became the next question, and it certainly did not seem to have an easy answer.

A committee again was picked in due course, and much to Marty's chagrin, Clark was named to be the chairman. The committee asked for a meeting with the pastor, at which time the men hoped to discuss quite openly with Reverend Knutson how the people felt.

Reverend Knutson showed no surprise or concern at being asked to meet with the men, but the meeting itself had its touchy moments. The reverend seemed to think the meeting had been arranged to offer him commendations, and perhaps to even suggest an increase in his rather modest salary, modest by his standards at any rate.

He was noticeably taken aback when the meeting took a different turn.

The reverend was not only well educated himself, he informed the little group, but he was also dipping into the writings of other highly trained theologians. His sermon material came directly from the greatest minds of Christendom. He could show them chapter and page.

The good reverend found it hard to fathom that anyone would not highly favor his intellectually charged sermons. He'd had no idea when he accepted their call that the people of the area were so bereft of learning and so insensitive to spiritual enlightenment. But he was sure he could do better. He knew of a great scholar whose books had just been made available, and though they were full of exceptional material, they were written in the "easy language of the layman." He'd send for a couple of those books. He was sure the congregation would find encouragement and religious sustenance in the works of this great man.

It was with great difficulty that the committee, Clark in particular, was able to convince the reverend that they wished him to end his service to them as their minister.

Clark explained it thus: "Reverend, we realize thet ya are a very learned man, an' we realize thet we are a mite slow. We wouldn't want to hold ya back from preachin' to those who could understand and appreciate yer great skills, so we are releasin' ya to go back to wherever ya wish to go, an' at such time as ya are first able to make the arrangement."

The reverend, red-faced, sputtered around, trying to formulate his response. "Are you saying, gentlemen," he finally choked out, "are you saying that my service has been terminated?"

"Shucks, no," put in the elder Coffins, another committee member, "not terminated, jest excused."

So they excused the parson, gave him a going-away purse, wished him well, and got on with the job of selecting a new minister. This time the schoolteacher, Mr. Wilbur Whittle, was not asked to serve as correspondent.

———

As yet the cemetery beside the little church stood empty of markers. They all knew it could not remain so, and the unasked question often hung in the air—*who?* Who would be the person whose passing would cause the ground first to be broken that they might be laid to rest?

Without conscious thought, various ones observed their neighbors. Grandpa Stern was well on in years and seemed to be failing. Mrs. LaHaye had never truly recovered her full health. One of the Coffin girls seemed very delicate and was always down with one sickness or another. Her parents didn't even allow her to go to school. Mrs. Vickers showed signs of high nervousness, and some feared she'd talk herself right into an early grave.

But when it happened it was none of these, and the whole community was shaken by the suddenness and the sadness of it all.

It was their own Tessie, who recently had married Mr. Whittle. She had always seemed like such a strong, healthy girl, and the community folk were pleased when it was known she was going to make her schoolteacher husband a father. As for Mr. Whittle himself, his bowler hat had never been dusted more frequently, his giant mustache been trimmed with more care, nor his spats whitened with such vigor. He was well pleased with himself and his new wife. To have a young and attractive woman adore him was a wonder in itself, and to be about to become a father was beyond belief. Mr. Whittle was on cloud nine. The big boys joked among themselves that his voice was now always squeaking with excitement, but Mr. Whittle did not seem to notice or care.

The great day came and the doctor was quickly sent for. With tired eyes and a heavy heart, he left the next morning.

Both Tessie and her baby boy had died during the night. The news shook the whole community. The neighbors responded with deep care and sympathy, and several gathered to dig the grave in the new cemetery. A pine box was built and carefully draped, and the two bodies, one so tiny, were prepared for burial. Through it all Mr. Wilbur Whittle moved in silent shock. It was beyond his comprehension, this great loss. In the absence of a parson, Mr. Whittle did have presence of mind to ask Clark if he'd read the Scripture and say the words of interment. Clark, with a heavy heart, agreed.

The day of the funeral was cold and dreary. Marty, wiping her eyes, thought the weather matched the occasion. The pine box was lowered, the earth heaped upon it.

She stood gazing at the fresh grave that held a young mother with a baby boy in her arms. *It's no longer virgin—this cemetery. From now on it will be grave added to grave,* she thought numbly. Time and again the earth would be opened up to receive a new burden.

Oh, Tessie, Marty cried inwardly, *who would've thought it would be you! Life is full of the unexpected.* And once more her thoughts went back over the years to another gravesite and her own loss. She lifted Ellie into her arms and held her tight, thanking the Lord for His goodness to her and to Clark in spite of the tragedies of life.

Classes were canceled until further notice, but Mr. Whittle was never able to resume his teaching, so school for that year ended in April. Toward the end of May, when the roses were beginning to bloom and the birds were rebuilding their nests, Mr. Whittle gathered a bouquet of wild flowers and placed it on the new mound of earth. Then dusting his bowler hat, he picked up his suitcases and returned to the East.

TWENTY-SIX

Josh and Nandry

The parson's departure left two members of the congregation particularly concerned. Josh and Nandry were worried about what this would do to their wedding plans. Clark picked up on what they must be thinking and did some investigating on his own.

He discovered there was a parson two towns away, and he visited the man and made arrangements for him to be at their community church on the day set for the wedding.

When he felt quite confident that nothing would happen to put a hitch in the plans, he opened the subject to Josh and Nandry one day when the two were sitting at the kitchen table with rather concerned expressions.

"This here weddin' ya been plannin'—ya changed yer minds 'bout it?"

"Oh no," Nandry said, looking to Josh for support.

"Gonna be a bit tricky without yerself a preacher."

Josh agreed, looking down at his hands folded in front of him. Nandry seemed about to cry, a thing she had never been known to do.

"Jest so happened," Clark went on in a rush, the teasing now gone from his voice, "thet I heard of a man within ridin' distance who also happens to be a church-recognized parson."

The two faces turned as one to focus intently on his.

"Where?" asked Josh. "Do ya think we could go to 'im?"

"Reckon there ain't much need fer thet," Clark said calmly. "He said he'd be happy to come on over here."

Nandry sat silently, her eyes wide, then rose with sudden comprehension and an exclamation of joy.

"Are ya sayin' thet ya found us a parson?" she cried, her hands clasped tightly together.

Clark grinned. "Thet's 'bout it, I guess."

"Oh, bless ya!" Nandry squealed. She looked about ready to throw her arms around Clark, then turned quickly to embrace Josh instead. Josh didn't mind.

Marty smiled from her place at the cupboard, remembering Nandry's early crush on Clark and so glad to see her genuine love for Josh.

Her attention was drawn back to the happy couple and the grinning Clark.

"When?" begged Nandry. "When can he come?"

"Well, I thought as how you'd set yer mind on May twenty-eighth."

"We did—we have. Ya mean we can have the weddin' jest as we planned—in the church—with our friends?"

"Yup—jest as planned."

"Oh, thank the Lord!" said Nandry. "He does answer."

The two young people left for a walk down by the creek, no doubt to share this moment of happiness and to finalize their plans.

"Well," said Marty, her own happiness filling her heart, "how did ya ever manage this bit of happy cunning?"

"Didn't take no cunning," Clark answered. "Jest money." They couldn't help but laugh together.

The much-planned-for wedding came off as scheduled. The hired parson did a commendable job of reading the vows and instructing the bride and groom.

Nandry was glowing and even lovely in her special gown she and Marty had carefully stitched for the occasion, and Clae looked almost as pretty as she stood beside her sister.

Josh's younger brother, Joe, stood with him. It was a beautiful wedding ceremony full of meaning and promise, and when the guests turned from the service to the bridal supper, there was much laughter and good-natured banter.

"Here ya are," Todd Stern joked to Clark, "hardly dry behind the ears yet, an' already givin' a girl away."

Clark looked over at his young Missie, who was growing up all too quickly.

"An' 'fore I know it," he said quietly, "I'll be losin' thet one, too."

Clark's mood turned sober as he thought about it.

"Seems like yesterday I had 'em all stumblin' round under my feet," he said to Todd, "an' here I am on the edge of bein' a grandpa. Sometimes I wish thet time had a tail, so's we could grab ahold an' slow it down some."

Throughout the summer months the church remained without a pastor, but it did not alarm Clark and Marty or their neighbors to be left with a vacant pulpit. They were sure that in God's good time He would bring someone to them. They did continue to meet to sing, pray, and read the Scriptures together.

The school, too, had no teacher. A meeting of its governing board resulted in Clae being asked to take the position come fall. Clae could hardly believe her good fortune. Here she was, newly returned from her teacher training and already a school was promised to her—her beloved home school at that.

Marty couldn't help but be excited, too, about Clae's new job.

"It will be so good to have ya home agin. We missed ya so," she told Clae with a hug.

"You spoil me," said Clae slowly. "In a lot of ways I would love to live at home . . . but . . . well . . . I've a notion that I sort of want to be on my own. I really want to set up house-keeping in the teacherage. There are still dishes and everything there, and Mrs. LaHaye told me I could just move in and make use of them if I'd like. I'd really love to. You wouldn't mind, would you, Ma?" She looked a moment into Marty's face. "Besides," she hurried on, "I'm doing some studies by mail, and I'll truly need the quiet if I am to complete the course in the time allowed."

Marty was disappointed, but she hid her feelings from Clae, simply saying she and Clark would talk it over. After a long discussion with Clark, she reluctantly gave in. It wasn't like Clae would be off on her own, after all, Clark said. She would be just down the road and over the hill.

It was decided that Clae would move back in with Missie for the summer months to fill in some of the emptiness left by Nandry's departure. Then before the fall classes began, she would move her belongings into the teacherage and set up housekeeping on her own.

A few leads came in concerning a possible pastor. These were followed up, and one or two seemed to fit the bill. But eventually those doors closed. Not that the search committee was hard to please, but the few available for the post wanted more salary than the little community could provide.

It was getting on toward fall when Ben heard about a young man from Mr. Cassidy.

"He's from my former hometown," said the store manager.

"Young fella—not too much book learnin'—did get some trainin' but hasn't been on to seminary in the East like he's aimin' to do. Got lots of zeal, an' sure does study out of the Good Book—honest an' hardworkin', but green."

"We don't mind greenness none," Ben offered. "We's all pretty green ourselves—maybe we could learn together."

A two-man delegation left on horseback to see if they could track down the young man in question. It was eight days before they were home again, but they returned with good news.

They had located the man, and he was eager to begin pastoring. He still hoped to advance his education, but if they'd take him as he was, he'd do his best to serve them. They had agreed.

Pastor Joseph Berwick arrived on the fifth of September, the same day Miss Clae Larson began teaching her first classes in the country school. He would not be giving his first sermon until the following Sunday, but in the interim he began to call on his parishioners.

He would be boarding with the Watleys, as had his predecessor, and when Mrs. Watley laid eyes on the tall, handsome young man, she turned to her two daughters with a twinkle in her eyes. She nodded the parson into the parlor, where tea was served. "Surely this time," she said, sighing.

Parson Berwick was not content very long to sit and sip tea, and before the dust of his last horseback ride had had a chance to settle, he was off again to meet more of the inhabitants of the area whom he saw as members of his flock.

He was not above lending a helping hand, either, and he spent some time cutting wood for Widow Rider, helped pound a fence post that Jason Stern was placing, and forked hay along with the Graham boys.

Gradually he worked his way through the community toward the schoolhouse, and on Thursday around four o'clock he rode into the school yard for a call on the local teacher.

Clae, down on her knees in the neglected flower bed, was not prepared for visitors. Hair hastily pulled back with a ribbon, she was busy cleaning out the weeds that had been left to grow where they wished over the summer, and her hands were deep in the soil.

She looked up in surprise at the approaching stranger, involuntarily leaving a streak of dirt across her cheek as she tucked a loose strand of hair back.

"I'm Parson Berwick," the man said politely as he dismounted. "Is your father at home?"

Clae shook her head dumbly, trying to sort out who he might mean by her father and where she should tell him that he could be located.

"Your mother?"

"No . . . no one . . . I'm . . ." She took a breath and changed course. "You're meaning the Davises," she asked, "or the Larsons?"

It was the parson's turn to look confused. "I'm meaning the teacher," he said, "whoever he is. I haven't yet heard his name."

"There is no *he*."

"I beg your pardon."

"The teacher . . . he's . . . he's gone," Clae stumbled along, trying to explain. "He doesn't live here anymore."

"I'm sorry," said the parson. "I understood the children are at school, having classes."

"They are—we are," Clae quickly amended.

"And you are one of the pupils?"

Clae stood up to her full height, which probably didn't make much of an impression alongside the parson's tall frame.

"*I*," she said with emphasis, "am the teacher."

"The teacher!" he stammered, his face turning red. "Oh, my goodness!" he exclaimed. "Then I guess I must be wanting to see you instead of your father. I mean—I didn't really come to see him. I came to see the teacher."

After a pause, he chuckled with some embarrassment. "Let's start all over, shall we?"

He stepped back, then forward again with a boyish smile.

"Hello there," he said, holding out his hand. "I'm Pastor Berwick, new to your area, and I'm endeavoring to call on each of my parishioners. I understand you are the new schoolteacher hereabouts."

Clae looked down at her dirt-soiled hand, but the pastor did not hesitate. He reached for it, and Clae felt her hand held in a firm handshake.

"I'm sorry," she stammered. "My hands are dirty—"

"You've got dirt on your face, too," he said with a smile.

"Oh my!" said Clae, further flustered. She reached up to rub at the suspected spot, only to make it worse.

He laughed, and pulling out a clean handkerchief, he stepped forward with "May I?" and wiped the smudge from her face.

Clae held her breath. Her throat felt tight and her heart pounded. She wondered if Mr. Berwick could hear it.

"As I said, I'm calling on my parishioners," he said, stepping back and putting his handkerchief in his pocket. "Can I expect to see you in church on Sunday?"

"Oh yes," whispered Clae, feeling her cheeks grow hot at her foolishness.

"And you really are the schoolteacher?"

She nodded.

"Sure didn't have teachers like you when I went to school."

She caught the twinkle in his eye, and her color deepened.

"I'll see you Sunday."

She nodded.

He mounted his horse and was about to move on, then stopped and turned to her.

"You didn't give me your name."

"Clae—Clae Larson."

"*Miss* Clae Larson?"

"Miss Clae Larson."

"How do you spell that? Clae. I've never heard that name before."

Clae spelled it. She was so nervous she hoped she'd said the right letters.

"Clae," he repeated. "That's unusual. I'll see you on Sunday, Miss Larson."

She watched him ride away with a wave of his hat.

So it was that Clae met the new preacher, and so it was that she had problems concentrating. Right from the very first she had trouble keeping her attention on the sermon rather than the one who delivered it—but she never missed a Sunday.

TWENTY-SEVEN

A New Parson, a New House

Soon known as Parson Joe, their pastor quickly established his place in the community. His willingness to lend a hand certainly endeared him to the men.

"Not 'fraid to dirty his hands, thet one," commented a farmer.

"No—nor to bend his back" was the immediate agreement.

But the real reason for their nods of approval was the Sunday services. Parson Joe made a list of all the hymns the congregation knew by heart, and these were the ones from which he selected their Sunday songs. Occasional new ones were added and learned by writing the words on a chalkboard borrowed from the school. Parson Joe had a nice tenor, and the congregation joined him heartily.

His prayers were not just words but were filled with sincerity, and his sermons were the highlight of the whole service. Simple, straightforward messages, developed from a text or passage in the Bible, gave them all a real sense of being spiritually nourished.

Even the younger ones began to take notice and listen, and eventually young Clint Graham surprised his folks by announcing that he felt the call to go into the ministry.

Only Mrs. Watley felt any disappointment in the new

parson—and it had nothing whatever to do with his Sunday sermons. She was beside herself to discover how to make him pay more attention to one of her daughters—which one he chose, she didn't care, but the man seemed oblivious to both of them.

The congregation continued to grow both numerically and spiritually. Young Willie LaHaye never missed a Sunday, and even his father, Zeke LaHaye, put aside work for an occasional Sunday morning of worship. The loss of his daughter Tessie no doubt had softened the man. Marty noticed on more than one occasion his eyes on the silent mound across the churchyard. A carefully crafted cross had appeared at the gravesite bearing the words *Tessie LaHaye Whittle and Baby Boy. May their rest be peaceful and never alone.*

Parson Joe called on his flock more than for Sunday dinner, and wherever he went he was welcomed.

Claude Graham was overheard remarking to his twin brother, Lem, "The reason he fits here so well is thet he don't know nothin' from them books neither."

To which Lem replied, "Don't let him fool ya. He's got a lot more of a load up there than he's throwin' out each Sunday. No use forkin' a whole haystack to growin' calves."

As for Clae, she felt rather befuddled about the whole state of affairs. To get her mind off her confusion, she worked every spare minute on her mail-order education. The study course that normally should have taken until the next summer was completed by Christmas.

The parson was always friendly to her, but no more so than with each member of his congregation. Still, Clae couldn't stop the ridiculous skipping of her heart, the hoping that perhaps, just perhaps, he had noticed her and he was maybe just a bit more attentive to her than to some of the other young women.

At times she despaired; at other times she dreamed . . . if only . . . if only.

And then on Easter Sunday morning following a wonderfully inspirational service, the young parson held her hand just a bit longer as she left the church. She was the last one to leave, having stopped to pick up her chalkboard for its return to the school.

"Good morning, Miss Larson." He smiled, and then he whispered, "I do wish you didn't live alone. How in the world is a gentleman to call?"

Clae caught her breath.

Allowing what she hoped was a decent amount of time, Clae moved back home with the Davises.

————

Clark and Marty sat after breakfast enjoying a second cup of coffee. It seemed as though they rarely had the opportunity anymore for a long chat.

"Looks like we got us a real growin' church," Clark commented.

"Yeah, it's so good to see folks comin' out, giving themselves—"

"Thet isn't what I'm meanin'."

"Then what?"

"I noticed Nandry an' Tommie's Fran are both in the family way."

Marty smiled. She had noticed it, too, and Nandry already had shyly shared her happiness with Marty.

"Speakin' of growin'," Clark said after a moment, "I'm thinkin' thet we've put it off fer too long."

"Meanin'?"

"This house—it's way too small. Shoulda built another ages ago."

"Seems a strange thing to be thinkin' on now. Notice who's around here much, at least during daylight hours—jest you an' me an' little Luke. Soon he'll be off to school, too."

"Yeah," said Clark, "but they start out here every mornin' and come home agin every night, an' they don't usually come alone—iffen you've noticed."

Marty thought of Missie and Clare each showing up with a friend after school during the last few weeks. Arnie was a big boy like his pa, and he and Clark seemed to fill up any room they were in at the same time. Ellie, their little social butterfly, no doubt would also be inviting her friends home, too, during the coming years. Marty also thought about Nandry and Josh and their baby who was on the way. Then her thoughts moved to Clae and the young parson. And Missie was quickly maturing into a young woman; before long she would be entertaining her young men callers.

"Maybe yer right," she said, "maybe we do need a bigger house. It's jest thet it seems so quiet like when they're all off to school. This little house has been a cozy home for us, Clark." She reached across the table for his hand. "Thank ya again for—"

"It's me doin' the thankin', Marty," Clark said, squeezing her hand. "This was jest a roof over our heads till you came and made us a home."

Marty's eyes misted and her smile was a little wobbly at the corners. Then she said, "Yeah, we do need us more room. What're ya thinkin'?"

"I think I'll spend me the winter hauling logs," he answered. "This here new house—I been thinkin' on it a lot. Not gonna be a log one. Gonna be boards—nice boards."

"Thet'll cost a fortune."

"Not really. There's a mill over 'cross the crik now. I can trade my logs in on lumber. Been thinkin' on the style, too.

How ya feel 'bout an upstairs—not a loft but a real upstairs? With steps goin' up—not a ladder. Like them fancy houses back east."

Marty caught her breath. "Seems to me ya got pretty big dreams," she said carefully, not wanting to dash them.

"Maybe—maybe I have, but I want you to do a little dreamin', too. I want this house to have what yer wantin'. More windows, closets fer clothes 'stead of pegs—whatever yer wantin'. Ya do some dreamin' an' write yer plans down on paper. We'll see iffen we can't make some dreams come true."

"When, Clark?" Marty finally asked, feeling nearly overwhelmed with the possibility but also worried that it was too much.

"Not next year—I don't s'pose," he answered. "Gonna take a long while to git all those logs, but the year after—should be able to do it by then fer sure."

"Sounds . . . sounds . . . like a fairy tale," Marty said in wonder, finally accepting the fact that it really could happen.

Clark grinned and stood up. He reached out and touched her hair.

"Did I ever tell ya that I love ya, Mrs. Davis?"

"I've heard it afore," said Marty, wrinkling up her nose, "but it bears repeatin' now an' then." She caught his hand and held it to her cheek.

He tipped her face up to his, then leaned to plant a kiss on her forehead.

"By the way," he said, "thet's mighty good coffee."

Livin' and Learnin'

Missie had arrived at her last year in the local school under the supervision of Clae, and as her school days came to an end, Luke's would begin. Clae had promised the school one more term, and then it was hoped Missie would take over, for she, too, had decided to pursue teachers' training.

Clae, living again in the Davis home, clearly was not committed to a life in education, though she certainly made a fine teacher and her students loved her. Marty was sure that Clae would make a fine parson's wife. Though the Davis household got the lion's share of the young parson's calls, he did not neglect the rest of his parishioners. Only Mrs. Watley had any real difficulty with the frequency of his calls at the Davis household.

Marty could hardly bear the thought of Missie going away for further education. Somehow it seemed more difficult to face than when Clae left. Missie was a bit younger than Clae had been when she left, having started school at not quite six— Clae had been older when she began her schooling. But Marty knew she had to get herself mentally and emotionally prepared for the inevitable.

Clark spent the winter months hauling logs to the mill across the creek. He was well pleased with the progress he was making and could see no problem with scheduling and building the new house during the next year.

Nandry's baby girl arrived, and they named her Tina Martha after her *two* maternal grandmothers, Nandry said. Marty felt very honored.

"Well, *Grandpa*," she said to Clark as she held the soft little one, "we've got our feet in two worlds—parents and grandparents both." The family laughed and joked about it all, and Luke wondered what he should now call his ma and pa.

Fran and Tommie's baby arrived about the same time—a solid, healthy boy whom they named Ben and who immediately was Little Ben.

Sally Anne gave birth to her third child, but Little Emily lived only three days, and a tiny fresh mound was sorrowfully dug in the cemetery by the church.

Rett Marshall was now handling a team of horses almost as well as a grown man. He loved creatures, tame or wild, and even had a young jackrabbit for a pet. A strange boy, people occasionally noted, but there was admiration in their voices. Several farmers had hired his services when they needed a pair of strong arms and a way with animals.

Marty remembered an overheard conversation from long ago between a neighbor and the doctor. "I often wonder, Doctor," the woman had said, "do ya ever wish thet maybe ya hadn't . . . well . . . hadn't fought quite so hard like at the birthing of the Marshall boy?"

The doctor had looked at her a moment, then said evenly, "Of course not." He then went on to say, "I didn't make that life—the Creator did. And when He made it, I expect He had good reasons for doing as He did—and whatever that reason is, it is in His hands."

Marty thought of this each time she watched the boy whistle a bird down or make friends with a prairie dog. She thought of it, too, when she saw the love in Wanda's eyes and Cam's pride in his son.

The LaHaye farmstead no longer resembled anything that had ever belonged to Jedd Larson. Zeke LaHaye was a good farmer who knew land well. Under his care the fields produced and the farm prospered. New buildings and a new well grouped nicely under the trees. Neat rows of fencing encircled the holding. But for all the prosperity of the homestead, Mrs. LaHaye remained in poor health. Their son Nathan married a girl from town and moved her into the big house with the family. She was a pleasant girl and was able to take over much of the running of the household. This was a great source of comfort to the senior Mrs. LaHaye.

Marty sat in her rocker with another pair of Luke's torn overalls on her lap and thought about all the changes that were happening. New neighbors moved in. Very little farmland in the area now was not in use. New buildings sprang up in town, almost overnight it seemed, as new businesses were added. The town had built a church of its own and had brought in a pastor to care for the people. There was even a sheriff's office and a bank. A daily stage now ran between the local towns. All these developments made their small community feel no longer like they lived on the frontier. Why, they were nearly self-sufficient.

They had their church, they had their school, they had a doctor they could call on. Marty certainly didn't consider herself a pioneer woman anymore.

The next summer saw Clae and the young parson joined together in marriage. Instead of asking the town's parson to do the honors, the young couple went back east to his hometown. Parson Joe was anxious to introduce Clae to his family and also eager to have his former pastor and dear friend perform the ceremony. The Davises of course were sorry to miss the event, but they made plans for a community potluck supper to honor the couple upon their return.

The school board agreed to rent the teacherage to the pastor and his wife for a modest amount, and this was fine with Missie, since she preferred to live at home upon commencing her duties. She no doubt had realized the restrictions on her social life if she were to live alone.

———

In spite of a bad accident with an axe, Clark met his log quota the following winter.

He had been cutting logs alone on the hillside when the axe blade glazed off a knot and spun sideways, slicing deeply into his foot. He had bound his foot as best as he could, packing moss against it and tying it tightly with a strip of his shirt. He was trying to make it home on one of his new workhorses, Prince, when Tom Graham crossed paths with him.

Prince was not used to being ridden, and Clark'd had his hands full trying to handle the excited horse in his weakened condition. He had lost a lot of blood and was quite content to be helped from the skittish horse to Tom's wagon box, where he could lie down.

Tom pressed the horses forward in an effort to get Clark home as quickly as possible. He threw the harnesses on the fence, helped Clark into the house, and jumped on his own horse to go for the doc.

Marty nearly fainted at the sight of Clark. He tried to assure her that he would be fine, but his face was so white and his hands so shaky she wasn't convinced. Marty got him to bed, where she fussed and fretted over him, hardly knowing what should be done.

"If ya see no fresh blood," Tom had admonished over his

shoulder as he left, "best ya leave thet foot alone 'til the doc gits here."

Marty studied the foot for signs of fresh blood, but thankfully none seemed to appear.

"Could ya eat a little broth iffen I fixed it? You're gonna need strength, ya know." Being a woman, her thoughts went to nourishment.

At first it didn't seem to appeal much to Clark, but he nodded his head in the affirmative, then cautioned, "Not too hot—jest warm."

Marty complied. The time until the doctor got there seemed endless, but at last Marty heard a horse approaching. She stayed out of the room while the doctor cleaned and sutured the cut. A couple of times she heard Clark groan, and her knees nearly buckled beneath her.

"And you," the doctor caught her by surprise as she tried to busy herself in the kitchen, "you're almost as white as he is. You best sit you down and have a cup of hot weak tea with some honey in it." He sat her on a chair and found the items for the tea.

Doc handed her the cup. "It's going to take him a while, but he'll be fine. He's young and tough. He'll make it. Your big job will be to keep him off the foot until it has a chance to heal properly. I've a notion your job won't be an easy one. Can't you put him to mending or piecing a quilt?"

There was humor in the doctor's eyes, and Marty couldn't help but laugh. The thought of Clark sitting contentedly with a little needle in his big working hand, matching dainty pieces for quilting, was just too much. Doc patted her shoulder and laughed, too.

In spite of the deepness of the cut and the loss of blood, the foot healed neatly and quickly. Clare and Arnie very capably took over the chores, reporting it all to their pa when they came in to supper.

As predicted, Marty's biggest problem was to keep Clark down as the doctor had ordered. He grumbled and fussed at not being able to be up and busy as he was used to being.

Their new son-in-law, Parson Joe, came as often as he could for a game of checkers. He usually brought Clae along. Other neighbors dropped in now and then. They informed Clark that the logs already felled would be hauled to the mill before spring thaw, just as he had planned. Clark accepted their kindness with deep appreciation. And they, of course, remembered all the times he had put his shoulder to their plows when they were in difficult straits.

Missie brought books from the school for him to read, which helped him pass many hours.

Finally the long ordeal was over and Doc declared the foot healed enough to be stepped on again. Clark hobbled, but at least he was again on his feet—a fact that each member of the household was truly thankful for. Marty noticed that on some days his limp seemed to be a bit worse than others. *It must still bother 'im,* she said to herself. But when she asked him about it, he brushed off her concerns as of no consequence.

During the day the house was left to just Marty and Clark. First with Missie's semester away at teacher's training and now with Luke in school, rites of passage had been marked in the Davis family.

As soon as Clark was able, he was back at the logging again. The neighbor men, true to their word, had indeed hauled out all the logs he previously had cut, but according to his calculations, he still needed another four wagonloads.

Marty watched him leave every morning with a feeling of anxiety and breathed a silent prayer of thanks when he returned safely at the end of the day.

Marty was thinking about spring and the start on the promised new house. Having the actual construction begun would take on special meaning, for once it was started, it would mark the end of Clark's daily and solitary trek to the woodlands.

Marty watched as the new clapboard house took shape. It was even bigger than she had dreamed. There were windows in every room. A fieldstone fireplace graced not only the family living room and the parlor but their bedroom, as well.

Clark had obtained the services of two men from town to assist with the building, so that even when he was busy in the fields the work went on. Marty measured the windows and bought material for the curtains so they would be ready to hang when the house was completed.

The house would not quite be ready by fall, but they planned to celebrate their next Christmas in their new home. Nandry and Josh with little Tina, and a second new family member by then, as well as Parson Joe and Clae, would all be home to share the Christmas turkey with them. They could even stay the night if they wished, and no one would be tripping over anybody in unexpected places.

It was something grand to look forward to, and Marty spent many hours planning, sewing, and dreaming.

TWENTY-NINE

Missie's Callers

Missie closed the exercise book she had been marking and heaved a contented sigh. It was hard to believe she was already into her second year of teaching. She loved it. True, she had some rascals in her classroom, including her own young brother Luke, but all in all she was glad she had chosen to be a teacher.

She piled the books neatly together and got up to clean the chalkboard. Her back to the door, she screamed in alarm when a pair of hands suddenly circled around to cover her eyes.

"Hey, hey, it's okay," a voice said. "I didn't mean to frighten ya, only surprise ya like."

Missie turned to look into the face of Willie LaHaye. Through her mind flashed the dead mouse, the grasshopper, and other nasty pranks Willie had played in the past. Her fright turned to anger and she swung away in disgust.

"Willie LaHaye!" she exploded. "When are you ever going to grow up?"

She immediately wanted to bite her tongue, for her eyes assured her that Willie LaHaye had indeed grown up—at least on the outside.

Broad shoulders topped strong muscled arms showing inside his shirt sleeves; bushy sideburns indicated what his beard would be were he not clean-shaven, and Missie had to look up a good way in order to signal her wrath.

Willie only grinned, the same maddening, boyish grin.

Missie again spun around on her heel.

"Well, now that you've had your fun, you can just take yourself right on out the door. I'm busy."

"But I came to see the new schoolmarm," he said, seemingly not at all perturbed by her anger. "I think thet I could use a little help on my ABC's." He moved around to get in front of her.

"*A* is for apple, *B* is for bait," he recited. "*C* is for coyness— *E* is for Eve, and thet's about as far as I can git."

"You're not funny—besides, you missed *D*."

"*D,*" said Willie, "*D*—hmm. 'Bout the only thing I remember thet starts with *D* is—dear."

Missie was so angry she considered throwing the chalk brush she discovered was still in her hand.

"Willie LaHaye!" she started in sternly.

"I know, I know," said Willie comfortably, "I'm not funny. Actually I stopped by to give ya some good news."

"Such as—?" prompted Missie.

"Such as, I'm leavin'."

"Yer what?"

"I'm leavin'. I'm goin' on further west." Willie suddenly had turned very serious.

"To where?"

"Not sure. Ya know when Pa settled here, he'd been planning on goin' on further. Hadn't been fer Ma gettin' sick we would have gone on. Well, I always was a mite disappointed. I'd sorta like to see what's over the next hill. Pa's all settled in here now, and Nathan's married and settled in, too, an' I suddenly got to thinkin' they don't need me around a'tall."

Missie had cooled down some and was willing to talk if Willie would be sensible.

"What does your pa think?"

"Haven't told 'im yet."

"When would you go?"

Willie shrugged. "Don' know—that depends on a few things."

"Like—?"

"Like Ma—she's still not well, ya know, an' other things. Thought maybe next summer—maybe."

"Not soon, then?"

"Depends."

Missie turned back to her boards and finished erasing the day's lessons.

"How's the teachin' goin'?" Willie asked.

"Good," said Missie "—only I had to send Luke to a corner today."

"What'd he do?"

"He dipped Elizabeth Anne's ribbons in an inkwell."

"Spoilsport."

Missie remembered her own ribbons being dipped in an inkwell. And who had done it.

"It's not funny," she said, angry again. "Hair ribbons cost money."

"Reckon they do. I never thought about that."

"Well, I told Luke he had to save his pennies to buy new ribbons for Elizabeth Anne."

"You're a smart teacher."

"Not smart—just—"

"Pretty?"

"Of course not. Look, if you're not going to be sensible, I refuse to talk to you."

Missie walked over to close the open window. It was stuck—as usual.

"Here, let me help."

Willie stood directly behind her and reached out toward the

window. Missie was imprisoned between his arms. Her face flushed. She dared not turn around or she would be face to face with him.

Willie didn't seem in any hurry to lower the window, though looking at the muscular arms, Missie knew the problem wasn't his lack of strength.

"Can't you get it, either?" she asked, her voice surprisingly controlled.

"It's stuck, all right."

"Willie LaHaye!" she stormed, "you're a liar."

"Yeah," he said, grinning as the window came effortlessly into place. And there was Missie standing within the circle of Willie's outstretched arms.

Before Willie could make a further move, Missie ducked down under his arms, then stepped back a pace, her eyes flashing fire. Then she swung on her heel and grabbed her coat.

"Please see that the door is closed when you leave!" she threw over her shoulder and was gone.

———————

That fall Missie had her first caller. She sure didn't count Willie's visit to the schoolhouse as one. Marty knew this time in their daughter's life was bound to come, and soon. But even so, she was unprepared for it when it happened.

Missie had been the youngest member of her small class at the normal school for teachers. Though Missie never said so, she was a popular student, as well. Occasionally since returning home, Missie would refer to this fellow student or that fellow student, but Marty had not had any reason to feel that one was more special than the other. Then one day at the Davis door appeared a tall sandy-haired young man, well groomed and properly mannered. A large, beautiful horse, appearing to have some racing blood, stood tethered at the hitching rail.

"How do you do?" he began. "My name is Grant Thomas. Would Miss Melissa Davis be in please?" His voice was most respectful.

Marty stammered, "Why. . . why, yes . . . she's in." She finally found her tongue and her own manners. "Won't ya come in please?"

"Thank you. And are you Melissa's mother? She spoke of you often."

Marty was still flustered. "Thet's right . . . please step in. I'll call Missie . . . um . . . Melissa right away."

Missie seemed pleased to see the young man. Marty watched carefully for signs of more than just gladness at seeing an old school chum.

Grant stayed to share supper with them and proved to be a quiet, intelligent young man. Clark seemed to quite enjoy him, and Marty attempted to send Clark silent warnings that he shouldn't encourage him too much.

The two young people visited and laughed over the supper table, seeming to thoroughly enjoy each other's company, which made Marty feel funny little shivers of fear run through her. Missie was so young—only seventeen. *Please, please, Lord, I'm not ready to give our Missie up yet,* she implored.

Grant told them he planned to ride back into town before nightfall, and Missie saddled Lady and rode part of the way with him.

When she returned, Marty saw her go to the pasture gate to turn Lady loose, brushing and fussing over her before she sent her on her way. When Missie stopped outside at the basin to wash her hands, she looked quite normal enough. She paused on the porch to admire Ellie's cushion top that the younger girl was making before coming into the kitchen, humming to herself as she often did.

Marty had quickly picked up her knitting and was trying to

look and sound normal herself. "This here Grant," she began, "don't recall ya sayin' much 'bout 'im."

"Not much to say. Let's see . . ."

Marty could already see Missie's ploy coming: *Throw Ma off with some facts, nonessential facts, but facts, nonetheless.*

"He's three years older than me," Missie hurried on, "an only child; his ma leads the Ladies' Aid and his pa's a doctor. His folks live in a big stone house on Maple Street, I believe it is, only about seven blocks from the normal school. They like to entertain, so they have Grant's friends—which includes almost everyone—over for tea, or tennis, or whatever." She finished with a noncommittal smile.

Marty wasn't to be sidetracked so easily. "What I want to know is, are you one of Grant's friends?"

"Guess so."

"Special like?"

"Oh, Ma," Missie groaned, sinking to a chair nearby, "how do you make a fella understand that you like him fine—but it ends there?"

"Did ya tell 'im?"

"I thought I had done that before."

"An' this time?"

"I hope he understands."

Missie rose with a shrug of her shoulders and moved on to her room. Marty kept her knitting needles clicking. She must remember to speak to the boys and inform them that she wanted to hear no teasing about the young man who had called. She hoped the fellow truly did understand. Poor Grant. But she couldn't help but feel relieved.

———

Marty was not to be at peace for long, for Lou Graham asked Clark for permission to call. Marty had no problem with

Lou himself, but she still had difficulty accepting the fact that Missie was growing up. Nandry and Clae had both been older when they received their callers and married, and Marty had half hoped Missie would follow their example. Perhaps Missie would have, but several young men seemed to have other ideas.

Lou sat in their parlor now, he and Missie playing checkers. Marty noticed Missie deliberately attempting to lose. Missie was good at checkers and would never, without intention, be caught in the situation she was in now. Lou's mind didn't seem to be on the game, however, and he was not taking advantage of the opportunities she was presenting.

Clare, Arnie, and Luke found it most difficult to understand why Lou did not choose to join them in pitching horseshoes as he always had in the past. The three boys were finally sent to bed, still puzzling over the situation.

After checkers, Missie fixed cocoa and sliced some loaf cake. The adults were invited to join the young people at the kitchen table, and they found no difficulty in chatting with young Lou, whom they had known nearly all his life.

Missie walked with Lou to the end of the path from the road and waited as he untied his horse and left for home.

"Will he be back?" Clark asked Missie when she returned to the kitchen.

"I expect so."

Marty thought her voice lacked enthusiasm.

"Nice boy," she commented.

"Uh-hum. All the Grahams are nice."

"Do ya remember when ya were gonna marry Tommie?" Marty asked.

Missie giggled. "Poor Tommie. He must have been embarrassed. I told everybody that—but he never said a word."

"Well, thet's all long in the past," continued Marty. "Tom has his Fran now."

"And me?"

Marty looked up in surprise.

"That's what you're thinking, isn't it, Ma? What about me?"

"All right," Marty conceded, "what about you?"

"I don't know," said Missie, shaking her head. "I think I need lots of time to sort that all out."

"Nobody's gonna rush ya," Clark said, expressing both his and Marty's feelings.

Lou continued calling. Missie was friendly and a good companion, but Marty noticed she didn't show the bloom of a girl in love. Which was just fine by her.

THIRTY

Missie's Discovery

Missie was about to close up the school building when the door opened and Willie once more came in.

"Should I have knocked?" he asked.

"Wouldn't have hurt."

"Sorry," said Willie. "Next time I'll knock."

Missie continued to button her coat.

"Come to think of it—guess there won't be a next time."

Missie looked up then.

"I really came to sorta say good-bye."

"You're leaving?"

"Yeah."

"When?"

"Day after tomorra."

"You said you weren't going until summer."

"I said thet it depended on some things, remember?"

"I . . . I . . . guess so. Is your mother better, then?"

Willie shook his head. "'Fraid not. I don't think Ma will ever be better." There was sadness in his voice.

"I'm sorry," Missie said softly, then, "How are you going?"

"I'm takin' the stage out to meet the railroad. Then I'll go by rail as far as I can. Iffen I want to go on, I'll buy me a horse or a team."

"What are you planning to do once you get there—pan for gold?"

Missie's slightly mocking tone was probably not missed by Willie, but he chose to ignore it.

"Kinda have my heart set on some good cattle country. Like to git me a good spread and start a herd. I think I'd rather raise cattle than plant crops."

"Well, good luck." Missie was surprised that she really meant it, and she was also surprised by how much she meant it.

"Thanks," said Willie. He paused a moment, then said, "By the way, I have somethin' fer ya. Sort of an old debt like."

He put his hand in his pocket and came out with some red hair ribbons.

"Iffen I remember correctly, they were a little redder than these, but these were the reddest red thet I could find."

"Oh, Willie," whispered Missie, suddenly wanting to cry. "It didn't matter. I . . . I don't even wear these kinds of ribbons anymore."

"Then save 'em fer yer little girl. Iffen she looks like her mama, she'll be drivin' little boys daffy, an' like as not she'll have lots of ribbons dipped in an inkwell."

He turned to go. "Bye, Missie," he whispered hoarsely. "The best of everythin' to ya."

"Bye, Willie—thank you—and God take care of you."

Missie wondered later if she had really heard the soft words, "I love ya," or had only imagined them.

———

Missie tossed and turned on her pillow that night. She couldn't understand her own crazy heart. One thing she knew. She'd have to face up to Lou—tell him honestly and finally that she wanted him as a friend but nothing more. But even with that settled, her whirling thoughts and emotions would not let her sleep. She reached beneath her pillow to again finger the red hair ribbons. Crazy Willie LaHaye! Why did he have to trouble her so, and why did the thought of his leaving in two days bring such sorrow to her heart? Was it possible that after all these years of fighting and storming against him, she had somehow fallen in love? Absurd!

But Missie was not able to convince her aching heart.

The news came with the Coffin children at school the next day. Mrs. LaHaye had died during the night. Somehow Missie made it through her teaching duties. Her heart ached for Willie. He had dearly loved his mother. What would he do now? Certainly he would not be able to leave on the stagecoach on the morrow.

If only she had a chance to talk to him, to express her sorrow, and to take back some of the dismissive and sometimes downright unkind things she had said down through the years.

The school day finally drew to a close. Missie announced that due to the bereavement in the community, classes would be canceled for the following day.

That evening Lou came to call. It didn't seem quite right to Missie that a young man should go courting on the eve of a neighborhood funeral, and her agitation made it easier for her to follow through on her intention of putting a halt to the whole thing. Lou walked to his horse looking rather dejected.

The next day another mound was added to the cemetery by the church. Missie stood with the other mourners, the wind whipping her long coat around her.

When the others went in to be warmed by hot coffee, Missie left the group and walked toward a grove of trees at the far end of the yard.

She was standing there silently, leaning against a tree trunk, when a hand was placed on her elbow. She did not even jump. Perhaps she had been expecting, hoping for him to come.

"Missie?"

She turned. "I'm sorry, Willie—truly sorry about your ma." Tears slid down her cheeks.

Willie lowered his head to hide his own tears, then brushed them roughly away. "Thank ya," he said, "but I'm glad—sort of glad—thet I was still here. It could have happened after I'd gone, an' then—then I'd always have been sorry."

"Are you still going?"

Willie looked surprised at her question.

"Well, you said it depended on your mother, and I didn't know how you meant—"

"I didn't say thet—entirely. I said it depended on other things, too."

"On what?" The question was asked before Missie could check herself.

For a moment there was silence; then Willie said with difficulty, "On you, Missie—on you an' Lou. Guess ya know how I've always felt 'bout ya. An' now thet you an' Lou are . . . well . . . friends, there's nothin' much fer me to hang 'round here fer."

"But Lou and I aren't . . . aren't . . ."

"He's been callin' regular like."

"But it's over. There was never much to it—only friendship, and last night I . . . I asked Lou not to call again."

"Really? Really, Missie?"

"Really."

Another silence. Willie swallowed hard. "Would there be a chance . . . any chance thet I could . . . thet I could call?"

"You're crazy, Willie LaHaye," said Missie, laughing and cying as she reached up and put her arms around his neck. "Are you ever going to grow up?"

Willie looked deeply into her eyes, and he must have seen there the love he had hardly dared to hope for. He pulled her close in a tender embrace. Willie LaHaye grew up in a hurry.

THIRTY-ONE

Christmas Surprises

True to Clark's promise, the new house was ready before Christmas. The moving in was a big job, and on one of her many trips between the new and the old house, Marty told Clark she sure didn't want to do this again anytime soon. But once all the furnishings had been moved over and set in place, the new curtains hung, and everyone settled in their own rooms, Marty was well satisfied. Marty and Clark sat at the breakfast table with the first cups of coffee in their new place and thanked the Lord for His blessing on them and their family over the years.

"Well, the coffee is as good as ever. Sure relieved 'bout thet." Clark joked as he rose to go out to the barn.

Willie LaHaye was a frequent guest at the Davis's new home, and Marty and Clark both appreciated him. If they had to give up their Missie, they were glad it looked like it would be to such a fine young man.

But on Christmas Eve, Willie unintentionally broke into their sense of comfort and acceptance of the courtship. It was during a casual conversation with the men of the house. Nandry's Josh had been telling of his plans to get a better grade animal for his pig lot, and Willie stated this was the direction he wished to go—starting with a few really good cattle and gradually building his herd. But first he'd have to choose just

223

the right land for the project. He hoped in the spring of the new year to leave on a scouting trip and take plenty of time in picking his homestead. After he had secured it, he would return for Missie.

Clark went very still and Marty's head swung around.

"Yer not plannin' on farmin' 'round here?" Clark finally asked.

"I'm not plannin' on farmin' at all," Willie answered. "Got me a real hankerin' to do some ranchin' instead."

"How far . . . how far away ya think ya have to go to find good ranch land at an affordable price?" Marty asked hesitantly.

"Few hundred miles, anyway."

Marty felt weakness go all through her. Willie was heading farther west. Willie was also planning to marry her Missie. *Oh, dear God,* she mourned inwardly. *He's plannin' on takin' Missie out west.*

She slipped quietly out to the kitchen, hoping no one had noticed her leave. She walked into the coolness of the pantry and leaned her head against a cupboard door.

"Oh, dear Lord," she prayed again, mouthing the words through lips that trembled. "Please help 'im git this silly notion out of his head." Her head came up at a sudden thought. *I wonder, does Missie even know 'bout it?*

But Missie had followed her into the pantry. "Mama," she said, laying a hand on Marty's arm. "Mama, are you feeling all right?"

"I'm fine—fine," Marty assured her, straightening up.

"Is it . . . what Willie said?"

"Well, I will admit it was some kind of shock. I had no notion he had such plans."

"I should have told you sooner—"

"Then ya knew?"

"Of course. Willie talked about it even before . . . before we made any plans."

"I see."

"I should have told you," Missie said again. "I suppose Willie thought I had."

"It's all right, Missie."

"It's . . . it's kind of hard for you, isn't it, Mama?"

"Yeah . . . yeah, I guess it is." Marty tried to keep her voice from shaking.

"I suppose," said Missie carefully, "that you feel kinda like your own mama felt when you planned to leave with Clem."

Now, ya listen here, Marty wanted to admonish, *you're bein' unfair, throwin' thet up to me.* But after a moment she said instead, "Yes, I guess it is."

For the first time, Marty thought about her own mother's feelings and recognized why it had been so difficult for her own family to accept her leaving.

"Yeah," she said again, "I guess this is how she felt."

"But you loved Clem," prompted Missie, "and you knew you had to go."

"Yes. I loved him."

Missie put her arms around Marty and gave her a squeeze. "Oh, Mama, I love Willie so much. We've prayed about this together. We can go on farther west. We can open up a new land together. We can build a school, a church, can make a community prosper and grow. Don't you see it, Mama?"

Marty held her little girl close. " 'Course I see it. 'Course. It's jest gonna take some gittin' used to, thet's all. You go on back, now. Me, I'm gonna catch me a little air."

Missie looked a bit reluctant, but she turned back to the laughter coming from the family sitting room.

Marty wrapped a warm shawl closely about her shoulders and stepped out into the crisp night air.

The sky was clear and the cold emphasized the brightness of the stars above her. Marty turned her face heavenward.

"God," she said aloud, "she's yer child. We have long since given her back to you, Clark and me. Ya know how I feel 'bout her leavin', but iffen it's in yer plan, help me, Father . . . help me to accept it an' to let her go. Lead her, God, an' take care of her . . . take care of our little girl."

––––––

The Davises saw much of Willie LaHaye in the next few months. It seemed to Marty that he might just as well move in his bedroll. They liked Willie and approved of the relationship between him and Missie, but Marty knew their remaining time with Missie in their home would be far too short. After she and Willie were married . . . Marty tried to not even think that far ahead. But with Missie at school all day, it was difficult to be required to share her with Willie almost every evening.

Missie and Willie were full of plans and dreams. Willie spent much of his time talking to men who had been farther west, inquiring about good range land. He was advised by most to travel toward the mountains and then follow the range southward. The winter snows were not as deep there, was the consensus of opinion, and the range land was excellent. Willie was cautioned to make sure he chose carefully with a year-round source of water supply in mind.

One evening Missie returned from bidding Willie good night, but this time her eyes sparked and her cheeks were flushed with anger. She took a quick swipe at her cheek with the back of her hand in an effort to hide her tears.

Clark and Marty both looked at her in surprise but said nothing.

"That—that—Willie LaHaye!" Missie muttered and headed upstairs to her bedroom.

She did not tell them what the quarrel had been about, but two evenings later it appeared to be well patched up, forgiven, and forgotten.

On the tenth of May, Willie would be leaving to seek his new land.

Missie bade him farewell in private. His excitement carried over to her, filling her heart and imagination. She did want him to go find their land to fulfill their dreams, but, oh, she would miss him. And there was always the slight chance he wouldn't be coming back. She had heard tales of other men who had gone and, because of sickness or accident, never returned. He assured her, over and over, that he would return. She wanted to believe him and tried to shut out the black thoughts, but they refused to be thoroughly banished.

She knew that Willie, too, had wrestled with doubts. They had discussed many times the reality that the West was calling to him, but sometimes he wondered if maybe he was doing this all wrong. Maybe they should marry first and go together; then there would be no need for a separation. But then again it might be awfully hard on Missie—trailing him around looking for a place that could be theirs. Land was not as easy to come by now as it had once been—at least not good land. It would mean perhaps living in a covered wagon for many months. No, he had concluded, making her go through all that was selfish. He'd go alone first, then come back for her. Perhaps the months would pass quickly for both of them. He prayed that they would.

Willie also had talked frankly with Missie about the fact there were other neighborhood young men around—Lou Graham, for one—and Missie was a very pretty and appealing girl. Could a lonely girl, left for months on her own, hold on to the flame for him? Wait for him to return for her? She assured him, over and over, that she could.

Missie, who now walked beside him, her hand in his one more time before he left, put into words the thoughts of both of them. "It's going to seem an awfully long time, I'm afraid."

Willie stopped walking, turned her to him, and looked deeply into her eyes.

"For me, too." He swallowed hard. "I hope an' pray thet the days and weeks go quickly."

"Oh, Willie," cried Missie, "I'll pray for you every night . . . that . . . that God will keep you and . . . and speed your way."

"An' I fer you." Willie traced a finger along Missie's cheek, and she buried her face against his shoulder and let the tears flow freely. He held her close, and she could feel him stroking her long brown hair. A man wasn't supposed to cry, but she knew he was and loved him all the more for it.

It was time for Willie to go. He kissed her several times, whispered his promises to her again and again, then put her gently from him. He did not look back at her once he started for his horse.

"He'll be back," Missie promised herself aloud. "Willie will be back." And she lifted her face to the stars and whispered, "Please take care of him, Father."

———

Willie's good-byes were not yet over. Zeke LaHaye accompanied his son into town and puttered around at last-minute fixings and unnecessary purchases. When the time finally came for the group heading west to be off, Zeke stepped forward and gave his son a hearty handshake and some last-minute cautionary advice.

"Be careful now, son. Like yer ma woulda told ya iffen she still be here, be courteous to those ya meet, but don't allow yerself to be stepped on. Take care of yerself an' yer equipment.

It'll only be of use to you iffen ya look after it. Keep away from the seamy side of things—I not be needin' to spell thet out none. Take care, ya hear?"

Willie nodded, thanked his pa, and was about to turn and go when Zeke LaHaye suddenly cast aside his usual reserve and stepped forward to engulf his boy in a warm embrace. Willie returned the hug, acknowledging how good it felt to be locked in the arms of his father. The last thing Willie saw as he left was his pa, big and weathered Zeke LaHaye, brushing a tear from his sun-darkened face.

THIRTY-TWO

One More Surprise

It was a Saturday, and Marty was in the kitchen turning out a batch of bread when Luke skipped in.

Missie sat hemming a tablecloth and didn't even lift her head toward her young brother until he announced in a teasing, sing-songy voice, "Willie's comin'."

"Oh, Luke, stop it," said Marty. Missie was lonely and miserable enough without someone playing with her emotions. It had been nearly a year since Willie had left, and letters between them had been far too few. Not that either of them didn't want to write, but postal delivery to someone on horseback was difficult at best.

"He is *too* comin'—jest see fer yerself," Luke argued and pointed down the road.

Missie ran to the window. "He *is*, Ma!" she nearly screamed in her excitement and was out the door on the run.

"Well, I'll be." Marty stood at the window and watched Willie's galloping horse slide to a stop and the young man leap to the ground, all in one motion.

"I'll be," said Marty again. "The boy's been all the way west and back and then risks his neck in my yard." She smiled as she watched the young couple embrace, obviously caring not at all whether they had an audience.

Marty turned back to her bread. After he first had gone,

she had secretly looked forward to having extra time with Missie all to themselves. But the look in Missie's eyes and the evidence of sleepless nights soon made Marty realize that she, too, would gladly welcome Willie's return.

There was a lot of joy at the table that evening. Missie and Willie spent more time feasting their eyes on each other than eating. Marty couldn't help but hope maybe Willie's quest had been in vain and that he would settle for a farm in the area.

Finally Clark posed the question. "Did ya find what you're lookin' for out west?"

"Sure did."

Marty's heart sank, but she held on to her calm and kept a smile on her face.

"What's it like?" she made herself ask, surprised her voice sounded normal.

"Well, ma'am," Willie's eyes shone as he talked, "it's 'bout the nicest thing—landwise," he quickly amended with a grin toward Missie, "thet a man ever set eyes on." He turned back to the family as he continued, and Marty rose to replenish the bowl of potatoes.

"There's no tall timber in that area—only scrub brush in the draws. The hills are low and rolling with lots of grass. Toward one end is a valley—like a picture—with a perfect spot fer home buildin'. It's sheltered an' green, with a spring-fed crik runnin' down below. Lotsa water on the place, too. Three springs thet I know of—maybe more thet I didn't spot out yet."

The enthusiasm in Willie's face was contagious.

"Almost makes me wish I wasn't old an' crippled, son," Clark quipped.

Marty reached over his shoulder with the refilled bowl, then stood behind his chair and touched his hair affectionately. "I most surely am not married to anybody old and crippled, Clark Davis," she told him. "Who on earth are ya' talkin'

about?" The family laughed with her.

"Were ya able to make the deal?" Clark was a practical man. Searching out good land did not mean ownership.

"Thet's what took the time." Willie nodded. "Man, ya jest wouldn't believe the hassle—goin' here, goin' there, seein' this man, lookin' up thet 'un, sendin' fer government papers. I began to wonder iffen I'd ever git through it all."

He grinned and nodded again. "Finally did, though. The papers I hold declare it all to be mine. An' it's a lot closer to here than I'd expected it to be." Marty could tell he was stating this mostly for her benefit. "Won't take too long at all to travel on out," Willie told them. "There's a couple of wagon trains travelin' through thet way every summer. Takin' supplies mostly to the towns down south, but they have no objection to travelers followin' along with 'im. Thet way ya git there safe an' sound with all yer supplies at hand."

So it would be by covered wagon after all that Missie traveled. Marty remembered her own trip west by wagon and its tragic end not far from here. She had secretly hoped that if Missie really had to go, it could have been by train. She crossed to the fire and began adding wood where none was needed but soon checked herself. She'd be driving everyone from her kitchen with the heat.

No use trying to pretend anymore. Their beloved Missie would be leaving, going west, and in a very short time. Marty had not spoken out against it, but somehow she had pushed the idea aside, hoping that things would change—that the young couple would decide not to go. Now here was the excited young man, in possession of papers that declared him a landowner out west, and an equally excited Missie hanging on his every word as though she could hardly wait to get started. There was no stopping it now.

Marty decided to slip quietly out for a little walk to the spring.

———

As the wedding day drew nearer, the house was caught in the flurry of preparations. Besides the wedding itself, careful consideration needed to be given to each item Missie was collecting in preparation for her frontier home, for each one must be essential, must fit into the wagon, and would need to withstand the long trip.

Marty had gone to her old trunk and produced a lace tablecloth that had been made by the hands of her own dear grandmother for her wedding gift. Most of the things Marty had brought with her from the East she had long ago put to use, but this was special. Also in the trunk was a spread that Marty's mother had made. This would be saved for Ellie.

Besides sewing the linens and the various other household needs, Missie was busy preparing her wardrobe. There was no way she wanted to be caught short no matter how long they should be on the trail. Her dresses had to be light for the hot summer ahead and yet wear well during the rugged travel.

Missie sewed with enthusiasm. She enjoyed sewing, and with a purpose as exciting as this, the job was a pleasure rather than a chore. Bright bonnets and colorful aprons took shape. She crafted calico gowns, then bundled and packed them into stout wooden boxes that Clark had made. Marty kept thinking of things Missie would need. Things that she herself had not had the foresight to pack when she herself came west. Pans, utensils, kettles, crockery, medical supplies, jars, containers for food—the list seemed endless and often left Missie laughing with an "Oh, Ma."

Marty's anxious mind refused to find rest but continued to go over the same worn-out path again and again—no doctor,

no preacher, no schools, maybe no near neighbors—which meant no Ma Graham. Oh, how much she did not want to see Missie go.

But Missie sang as she worked and packed. The girl fairly danced through the house in her happiness.

———

At the sound of an approaching horse, Missie stood quickly from the machine, where she had been busy finishing a gingham dress.

"There's Willie. He promised me that he'd help me pick enough strawberries for supper. We won't be long, Ma."

Marty sighed and put aside her own quilting that also would be going into one of the boxes. She would make some shortcake to go with the berries.

The young people set off, arm in arm, for the far pasture, Missie's old red lunch pail swinging at Willie's side.

On the way to the kitchen Marty stopped and looked at Missie's sewing. She had become a good seamstress. Marty was proud of her.

She stood fingering the garment, and then her hand lovingly traveled over the machine. All through the years since she had become Missie's mama, this machine had sewn the garments for each of her children. Clothing was mended, new towels hemmed, household items for three brides had been made here, young hands had learned the art of sewing. It was a good machine. It had never let her down. True, it didn't have the same shine that it had when it was first carried through her door, but it had borne the years well.

Marty was deep in thought, and eventually her tears began to fall unattended. Then Clark was there beside her, and he reached out and took her hand. She looked up at him and

shook herself free from her reverie. It was a moment before she felt in control enough to speak.

"Clark, I been thinkin'. I'd like to give the machine—Ellen's machine—to Missie. Ya mind?"

It was silent for a time and then Clark answered. "It's yours to give. Iffen thet's what ya want, then it's fine with me."

"I'd like to—she'll be needin' it in the years ahead. And Ellen *was* her mama."

"An' so are you." His arm circled her waist, and she leaned against him.

"An' what will you do?" Clark finally asked.

"I can go back to hand sewin'. I was used to thet, but Missie—she's always used the machine. She'd be lost without it. 'Sides, I think thet it be fittin' like."

She brushed away the last trace of the tears, then reached out a hand to run it again over the smooth metal and polished wood of the well-loved machine.

"Will ya be good enough, Clark, to make it a nice strong crate, an' then I'll wrap an old blanket around it so's it won't get scratched."

Clark nodded his head. "I'll git right to it tomorra."

"Thank ya," Marty said and went to prepare the shortcake.

THIRTY-THREE

A Special Day

When Missie's wedding day dawned clear and bright, Marty felt it just suited the girl—their happy, excited, and pretty young daughter.

Marty paused a moment before leaving her bed to send heavenward a quick but fervent petition. *Oh, God. Please, please take care of our little girl . . . an' . . . an' make today a day thet she can look back on with joy and good memories.* She looked over at Clark still snoring softly and quietly slipped from under the covers.

There was much to be done. Marty knew she mustn't dawdle in sentiment or emotion. She dressed quickly and went to the kitchen. Clark soon joined her and built a lively fire in the old cook stove. When they had moved into the new house, Clark had told her she could have a new cook stove, something more up-to-date—but Marty had refused.

"Why, I'd feel disloyal," she had explained, "castin' out a faithful ole friend like thet. Thet old stove and I have boiled coffee fer friends, baked bread fer family, an' . . . an' . . . even cooked pancakes," she finished with a knowing smile, remembering her long-ago menu limitations.

So the old stove had moved with her. She checked the wood in it now and pushed the kettle forward.

Missie had decided to be married at home.

"I want to come down those stairs there on Pa's arm. Really, Ma, if you open up all of the rooms, it's most as big as the church anyway."

Clark and Marty had been happy to agree.

The morning hours flew by too rapidly. There were last-minute preparations of food for the afternoon meal. Fresh flowers needed to be brought in and arranged. Children needed to be checked to see that they had done their assigned chores. Marty felt as though she was on the run most of the morning.

The wedding was set for three o'clock in the afternoon. It was after two before Marty was able to hurry from the kitchen, do a last-minute check on the rooms, and run to her bedroom for a quick bath. Arnie had filled the tub for her. She then slipped into her new dress. Her long hair tumbled about her shoulders, and as she pinned it up, she noticed her fingers trembled. After a last quick check on her appearance, she went to Missie's room.

Marty thought Missie had never looked prettier than at that moment. Standing there in her wedding gown, her cheeks flushed, her eyes bright with tenderness, she looked so happy Marty's throat caught in a lump.

"Oh, Ma," Missie whispered.

"Yer beautiful, Missie," Marty whispered back. "Jest beautiful." She pulled the girl close to her.

"Oh, Ma," sighed Missie. "Ma, I want to tell you something. I've never said it before, but I want to thank you—to thank you for coming into our lives, for making us so happy—me and Pa."

Marty held her breath. If she tried to speak she'd cry, she knew, so she said nothing, only pulled her little girl closer and kissed the brown curly head.

Clark came in then and put his arms around both of them. His voice sounded tight with emotion as he spoke. "God bless,"

he said. "God bless ya both." He placed a kiss on the cheek of each of them, and then he placed his hand gently on Missie's head, tried to clear the hoarseness from his throat, and prayed in a low voice, "The Lord bless ya an' keep ya, the Lord make His face to shine upon ya and be gracious unto ya; the Lord lift up His countenance upon ya and give ya peace—now an' always, Missie. Amen."

Missie blinked away her tears and moved out into the hall to hear last-minute instructions from Parson Joe.

Clark reached for Marty. At first he said nothing, only looked deeply into her eyes.

"It hurts a mite, doesn't it?" he whispered.

Marty nodded. "Isn't she beautiful—our Missie?"

Clark's eyes darkened with emotion. "Yeah, she's beautiful."

"Oh, Clark—I love her so."

"I know ya do." He pulled her close and his hand stroked her back. "Thet's why yer lettin' her go."

Down below, the waiting neighbors were beginning a hymn. Marty knew it was time for her to take her place downstairs. Soon Clark would be coming down, too, with the radiant Missie on his arm.

She looked at Clark, silently accepting with deep appreciation the strength he offered. Then she slipped away.

She would not cry anymore—not today, Missie's wedding day. There would be many times ahead for that. Today she would smile—would face her neighbors as the happy mother of the bride—would welcome, with love, another son.

She stopped at the top of the stairs, breathed a quick prayer, took a deep breath, and descended smiling.

FROM *the* HEART *of the* PRAIRIE *to* YOUR HEART!

A BREATHTAKING NEW SERIES FROM A TWO-TIME CHRISTY AWARD FINALIST!

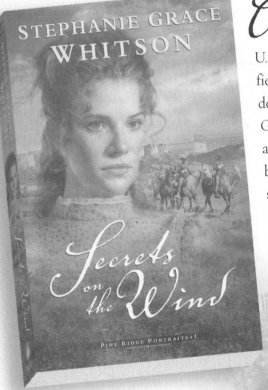

*O*n the desolate plains of frontier Nebraska, two U.S. soldiers discover a terrified woman in the cellar of a devastated farmstead. Laina Gray is taken to their post at Fort Robinson, where the best efforts to uncover the secrets of her trauma all fail. After living through her worst nightmare, is there any way she can learn to trust again?